FALLING FOR A HOOD KING

SHVONNE LATRICE

ABOUT THE AUTHOR

Other Works by Me:

Good Girls Love Thugs 1-5
Falling for a Hood King 1-4
Married to a Distinguished Thug 1-3
She's Gotta Have It 1-2
Me & My Dope Boy 1-3
Yazir & Nina 1-3
Forbidden Love with a Thug 1-3
You Needed Me 1-3
Shorty is in Love with a Real One 1-4
I Got Your Back 1-2
My Baby Is a West Coast King 1-4
Our Love Is the Realest 1-3
She Got It Bad for a Heartless Gangsta 1-4
She Got It Bad for a Heartless Gangsta: An AK Christmas
Hood Boyz Fall In Love Too 1-3
Nobody Can Love You Like Them Roughnecks Do 1-4
She Gave Her All to the Hood's Finest 1-5

Visit www.theshvonnelatrice.com for paperbacks!

facebook.com/ShvonneLatrice
twitter.com/siobhannoir
instagram.com/siobhannoir

$11.99
ISBN 978-1-966375-05-0

NATALIA THOMAS

"Would you like the $73.50 back on a gift card or cash, sweetie?" the cashier asked.

"Cash please," I smiled. She smiled back, and tapped her screen to make the drawer pop open.

"There you go. Is there anything else I can help you with?" she smiled.

"That's it. Thanks," I smiled and rushed out.

This was my usual routine. I would buy one cheap thing, then buy one expensive thing, switch the price tags, and return the cheap item to get the money from the expensive item back. I learned this from my mother Dalia. She was a full-blown scam artist, and it's pretty much how we got by every day.

My mother had me at 15 years old, and she had to do what she had to do to make sure we ate. I wouldn't necessarily say she was a good mom, but she was straight. You see, my father was the love of her life, but he got murdered. That was normal here in Indianapolis. Niggas got killed every day, and it never really shocked people anymore.

I was an only child, because every time my mother got pregnant by one of her new niggas, she had it scraped out. She said I was her first and her fucking last; her words, not mine. My mom was more like my sister who let me live with her. We lived separate lives, and anything I needed I had to buy it. That included, clothes, shoes, food, school supplies, a phone, anything I needed to get by these days.

My return scheme had gotten me plenty of things I needed from the thrifty clothing shops. I was nowhere near the best dresser, which is one reason I hated high school. My school was a damn fashion show, and if you didn't rock the newest Jordans, or jeans with a known label on it, you got clowned.

Only reason I wasn't completely miserable was because I was pretty as fuck. I had long, curly, chestnut brown hair, peanut butter skin, a naturally flat stomach, sexy legs, and a nice size ass. I had B-cups up top, but I was still proportioned. I didn't have one of those video model asses, but I def had one that made niggas' mouths water. I had dark brown eyes, long eyelashes, and a perfect set of white teeth that I thanked God for. Lord knows braces were not in the budget.

Niggas loved me and wanted to fuck, and they knew making fun of me was not the way to get some pussy. I was a virgin but I made niggas think otherwise, so that it seemed as if they had a chance to fuck me. It's not like I was waiting or anything; it was just that I had yet to meet a nigga to peak my interest. I was starting to think I needed to leave Indiana to find someone decent.

Another reason I could withstand the fashion school war was my best friend Lucy. She wasn't rich either, so she had to take some of the rare verbal abuse right along with me. She depended on her poor ass mama to take care of her, so sometimes I would have to buy her some $5 or $10 jeans when all her current ones had become capri pants.

I only had two more years left in that hellhole, including this one I was in. I swear, I couldn't wait to be 18, cause being 16 was some straight bullshit.

I smiled on my way to Lucy's house, cause I was $73.50 richer, and got to keep my new jacket I bought. $73.50 was just enough to buy me a $3.00 pack of panties, some pads so I could stop using toilet paper in their place, get lunch for the week, and pay my phone bill. I had an iPhone 4S, so not the newest, but it worked perfect. I bought it off eBay for $40.

"You look cute," Lucy commented, as she walked out of her house. I had on skinny jeans, some black, off-brand sneakers that I got from K-mart, and a black t-shirt. My curly hair was hanging down my back, and I had my black backpack on.

"Thanks. Let's go," I said.

"It's only 7:45, why you rushing? School starts at 8:15," Lucy frowned as she walked down her porch steps.

"Cause I want some breakfast from Burger King," I spat.

"Where you get money for Burger King?' Lucy asked.

"I hit up Oscar's early this morning," I smiled, and Lucy shook her head. "Don't shake your head! I bought those jeans you wearing with that good money!" I smiled. Okay, I wasn't all the way honest with y'all. A lot of times, I flat out stole clothes as well. However, stealing was a little more risky in my opinion.

"You gon' get caught!" Lucy chuckled.

"Sike!" I jerked my neck back. I had been doing this for over a year now, and never got caught.

We arrived to Burger King, and I ordered breakfast for Lucy and I. I was so hungry, cause I hadn't ate at all yesterday. My stomach was hurting so bad that I could barely sleep. I ended up eating ice, and drinking sugar water. That seemed to be enough to help me drift off to sleep.

Lucy and I sat down at a table to wait for our food. After a couple minutes, the employee called my name to let me know it was ready.

"Lucy, you gon' have to start finding a way to get cash," I said. I didn't mind buying her shit, but I could barely take care of myself.

"I'm 16, how am I gon' get money?" she asked, eating a piece of hash brown.

"You can do what I do, since I know your mom won't let you work," I said, squeezing the ketchup on my food.

"I ain't doing that shit you do, Nat," she spat.

"Well you need to figure something out, because I don't have much money this weekend," I said. I felt like we were married. Shit, I was 16 too; why did I have to always pay our way, or steal us new outfits?

She didn't respond, and sipped her orange juice. We ate in silence for a moment, until I heard loud talking, gum popping, and high heels.

"Damn Natalia, can't even afford Keds?" this bitch named Ratishay laughed.

"Still can't afford butt injections, Ratishay?" I fake smiled, referring to her obviously flat ass. She rolled her eyes and switched over to order her food. "I can't stand that bitch!" I said to Lucy, while watching Ratishay.

"Me either, you would think after you beat her ass, she would get the hint," Lucy said, glaring at Ratishay and her friends.

We finished our food and headed to school. I hated school with a passion, but I knew I needed to finish if I wanted to do something with my life. I couldn't be a petty thief forever. I would love to just wake up, and see a paycheck direct deposited into my bank account.

I finally got home to the apartment I shared with my mother, and I was exhausted from school. I didn't feel like dealing with my mom, especially cause I was on my cycle. *My cycle! Fuck!* I thought. I pulled my key out the door so I could stop by CVS for some pads. I wish I could wear tampons, but for some reason I couldn't get it up there. Lucy said once I started fucking, it would work. Lucy killed me; she was fucking, drinking, and smoking, but wouldn't steal.

I finally got to the store and stopped to catch my breath, since I'd ran the whole way. I walked in, and opened the small freezer to grab a water bottle. I downed it, and then hid the empty bottle behind some beer cans so no one would find it. I looked up at the aisle signs to see which aisle the pads would be on, and once I found it, I walked over and saw it was $8.00 for the Always brand. I shook my head and grabbed the CVS version instead. I picked up a small box of wipes, and headed to the register.

"$7.63." the cashier said non-chalantly. She clearly didn't want this job.

I pulled out my cash, and saw I only had $55 left after buying Lucy and I breakfast and lunch.

"Here you go," I said, handing the cashier a ten-dollar bill. "Where is your bathroom?" I asked, putting the change in my backpack.

"Straight to the back. Make a left," she said.

"Thank you," I replied, and grabbed my bag of pads.

I found the bathroom, and it was disgusting; not like I had to pee, but still. I didn't want this nasty aroma touching my bare vagina. I tried to lock the door, but realized it was broken. I blew out hot air, and wondered if I should wait until I got home to put on a pad. I decided against it, cause I felt myself soaking the toilet paper currently in its place. *Hurry up!* I told myself as I pulled my pants down, and began to remove the soiled tissue paper. I wiped myself clean with one of the wipes, and then opened the pad. Just as I was placing it in the crotch of my panties, someone busted in.

"I'm in here!" I yelled with my panties and jeans around my knees.

"Ugh! Nasty bitch!" the girl frowned and walked out.

I hurried up and finished, then washed my hands. I stuffed my bag into my backpack, and then left the store. I was hungry, so I stopped at Jack in the Box for some $1 tacos, curly fries, and iced tea. I shook my head at my dwindling funds and headed home.

"Aye little mama!" some nigga smiled, flashing his golds. I ignored him and kept walking since my house was near. "Aye little bitch! I know you heard me!" he yelled.

It was dusk, and I knew he would kill my ass right here and no one would tell. I started to run as I held tightly onto my iced tea, hoping it wouldn't slip. I made it to my complex, and rushed inside. Once I reached my apartment, I rushed in and slammed the door.

"Don't slam my fucking door!" my mother yelled.

"Sorry!" I yelled back, and plopped down on the couch. I turned on the TV, and saw it was some Love and Hip Hop LA re-runs on, so I selected it.

"Un uhn, you ain't pay to watch TV miss lady!" my mother walked out from the back with her hand out. I rolled my eyes, and went into my pocket. Yes, my mother charged me to watch cable and use the house phone. I usually would do it behind her back, so it was rare that I had to pay up.

"Here," I said slamming the $3 in her hand.

"Thank you. Why you ain't bring me shit to eat, Natalia?!" she frowned.

"I didn't have enough. Plus you just took my last $3," I lied. I could never ask her for money or food, but she stayed asking me.

"Whatever bitch," my mother shook her head. See, I told y'all my mother was more like my sister than my mother. She never spanked me as a kid, and always let me do what I wanted, when I wanted. She would beat your ass if you fucked with me though.

My phone buzzed, and I saw it was a text from this guy at school named Frank. Frank was fine, and in 12th grade. He was dark-skinned, tall, and on the basketball team. I didn't like him, but I knew he had cash, and I wanted it. I loved texting him, cause we always talked about sex. I liked to talk about it, but I didn't actually want to do it. I told him all kinds of made up sex stories, and he believed it. I just retold the ones I heard my mother telling her home girls when she was on the phone.

Frank: I'm so horny right now. Thinking about you.

Me: Thinking about me throwing it back?

I ain't know shit about throwing it back until I saw it on urban dictionary.

Frank: Damn, yes. What you doing right now?

Me: Eating. I'm on my period though.

Frank: I can still fuck.

I frowned and locked my phone up. He was too sexy to be that damn thirsty. Texting on my phone made me realize I didn't have enough for my phone bill this month. I had budgeted everything in my head, except Lucy's lunch and the $3 I just paid to watch Love and Hip Hop. I closed my eyes and exhaled heavily.

"Dalia, can I borrow some cash?" I asked.

"For what?" she frowned.

"My phone bill. I'm short $30," I lied. I was short $10, but I needed some cushion.

"When the fuck am I gon' get it back?" my mother frowned.

"End of the week," I replied, hoping I could make good on that.

"Aight Natalia, I want my damn money by 12 midnight," she raised a brow, and I smiled and nodded. She chuckled and reached into her purse. "You need to find work, CVS is hiring," she added as she handed me the money.

"CVS? I don't want to work there!" I frowned.

"No choice. The manager and I are good friends, and he said he'd give you a job working 4 to midnight," my mother spat.

Good friends meant she was fucking him. My mom was only 31 years old, but looked 25. She had long, straight, dark hair, flawless mocha skin, and a thick body with a nice size ass and big breasts. I wondered why I didn't get her breasts.

"Dalia!" I whined. My mother made me call her by her first name.

"Natalia!" she mocked me as she pulled a TV dinner from the freezer. "You start next Wednesday. Don't fuck this up, mommy needs him," she smiled, and placed her food in the microwave.

"Who did you tell him I was to you?" I asked, just to make sure we had the same story.

"My little cousin," she replied and I nodded.

NATALIA

TWO WEEKS LATER

I hated this fucking job, but I knew if I quit, my mother would kick my ass. The manager she was fucking was bringing in a nice amount of cash. He was the district manager, which sounded like he was the big dog around this area.

"You gon' be okay over here?" my co-worker Victoria asked, popping her gum.

"Yeah, I will be cool," I replied, looking at the time. It was 10 p.m., so I had just two more hours.

"Aight, I'm gon' go to the back and clean the aisles. When I come back, you can go to break," Victoria replied.

"K," I said, and started flipping through a magazine.

It was late, so no one was really in the store. Just as I was happy about it being so quiet, I heard a bunch of male voices in the distance. I rolled my eyes and put the magazine down. A group of five guys and two girls strolled in, laughing and talking. I picked the magazine back up and tried to focus on it.

"Damn are y'all still open?"

I looked up and saw some light-skinned guy with braids.

"Yeah. I'm here, ain't I?" I replied, turning my lip up.

"Well ring me up then! Mean ass!" he spat, and placed a bottle of Gin on the counter.

"ID please?" I asked. I wasn't allowed to sell alcohol, but I felt bold in this moment.

"You don't need no fucking ID! Ring my shit up so I can bounce!" the guy yelled.

"I ain't ringing shit up until I see some ID, nigga," I replied, standing my ground.

"Aye, chill out ma," some guy said, walking up. He was about 6 foot even, and had a fresh fade. He wore a black polo, dark blue jeans, and some Jordan Retro 7's. I didn't reply, because his sexiness made me completely forget about this current altercation. His peanut butter complexion matched mines perfectly, and his full lips made my mouth water.

"She asking for some fucking ID!" the annoying nigga yelled at me.

"You need to show ID when you buy liquor!" I frowned.

"Here!" some girl walked up, and handed me hers. She was light-skinned, with long red hair. She looked like a damn clown, but a pretty one. I looked over her ID, and could tell it was a fake. I had enough fake ones myself. I accepted it anyway, and charged them for the liquor.

The sexy guy in the black Polo, stared at me with lust-filled eyes. I smiled at him, until I saw the red head lean up and kiss his lips. *Of course, the one fine nigga in Indiana is taken.*

"Here is your change," I smiled. The annoying dude snatched his money from me, and stormed out.

"Thank you, Natalia," the sexy one said.

"How did you know my name?" I asked. He pointed to my nametag and chuckled. I was embarrassed as hell. Here I was thinking this was some romantic moment.

"Julius! Come on baby!" the red head yelled, and he left.

"Julius," I smiled to myself, and watched him leave.

I walked outside of CVS, and took a deep breath. Getting off work was the best feeling in the world. I would much rather go back to stealing and scheming though - not such long hours.

As I was walking home, an all-black 2016 Lexus pulled up on me. The windows were dark, and "Only Right" by Ty Dolla $ign was blasting. I sped up, hoping they weren't trying to rape and/or kill me.

"Slow down, Natalia!"

I turned around to see Mr. Sexy. "Julius?" I smiled. My smile once again faded when I spotted Jessica Rabbit in the passenger seat, rolling up.

"You need a ride, babe?" she asked.

"Nah, I just have a couple more blocks," I said, holding tightly onto my backpack straps.

"Girl! It's after midnight, and you're pretty as hell. Get in the car!" she shook her head, and pointed to the backseat with her thumb. She licked the blunt, as I entered the backseat.

As soon as I got in, Julius sped off from the curb. I instructed them on how to get there, and then hopped out quick as hell.

"Nice meeting you, Natalia. I'm Bianca," the red head said, extending her hand out the window.

"Nice meeting you too Bianca," I replied, shaking her hand.

"Bye Natalia," Julius said, licking his lips seductively. Bianca was still looking at me, so she didn't see. I half smiled at him, and ran inside my apartment complex.

NATALIA

"He was so sexy!" I beamed to Lucy.

We were in my room chilling. It was Saturday afternoon, and as a little gift to me from my mom's boo, I had Saturdays and Sundays off.

"Julius you say?" Lucy smiled, and I nodded. "You gon' finally let him pop that cherry?" she smiled.

"Hell no! He has a girlfriend, and she is really pretty and nice. Plus, even if he didn't, I don't know him well enough," I replied.

Lucy was a straight up slut in my eyes. All you needed to have was a nice amount of cash and a car, and she was fucking you. I can't tell you how many abortions I've had to save up for to help her.

"You gon' be a virgin forever!" she rolled her eyes, and scrolled on her unknown android.

"So! Sex ain't all that," I replied.

"Yes the fuck it is. Nothing like busting a nut on a nice thick dick," Lucy smiled.

"Ugh, please. I don't want to bust anything on nothing!" I turned my lip up as if sex disgusted me. Getting "wet" as they called it sounded nasty as hell, unless I was freak texting. Lucy rolled her eyes, and playfully bounced on an imaginary dick. "Stop Lucy!" I laughed hard as fuck.

"I need $20, Nat," Lucy said in a more serious tone.

"For what?" I frowned and sat up.

"Some nigga burned me, aight," she replied, shaking her head.

"With what?" I asked.

"I don't know. My pussy burns when I pee, and when I googled it, it sounded like Chlamydia. I ain't got insurance, but I know I can get the medicine for it for $20 at the clinic," she said non-chalantly. That was another reason I wasn't trying to fuck. I mean, all you got were STDs and babies.

"I only got $20 left from my check, but I got you Lucy. Don't worry," I exhaled.

"Thank you!" she smiled, and hugged me tight.

It was around 9 p.m. at night, and I was headed to Oscar's Retail. I was gonna buy some $5 jeans, and get one of my $50 tags and its matching receipt, that I saved at home. I would switch the tags out at home, then return the $5 jeans for $50, turning my last $20 into $55. On top of that, I planned to steal an additional pair to keep for myself. See, Oscar's Retail really had no idea on what tags matched what, so it made it easy to switch them out. I got the tag-attaching gun off eBay, at the advice of my mom.

I walked in the store slow, and tried to stay under the radar. Anytime you wore a backpack into a store, people looked at you suspiciously.

"Welcome to Oscar's!" the cashier smiled.

I half smiled and headed straight to the junior section. I picked out a nice pair of jeans for $6, more than I budgeted for, but whatever. I grabbed a second pair, and headed to the dressing room. I made sure to fold the second pair flat, and put it under my shirt.

"How many items?" the attendant asked.

"One," I smiled, and twirled the hanger to show her.

She took a green placard down marked with a one, and handed it to me. I walked into the dressing room, and took off my sweats. I quickly removed the jeans from under my shirt, and put them on. I put my sweats back on top of them, and came out.

"Did you like them?" the same attendant asked.

"Yes, I will buy them," I replied, and handed her the one placard.

I waited in line and finally got to the register.

"$6.64," the associate told me.

I went into my backpack, and pulled out my wallet to pay. I handed her the exact amount and she processed it, then handed me my receipt and bag. As I was zipping my backpack, I heard someone yell.

"Hey!" I looked to see a security guard pointing at me.

"Ma'am, you need to pay for those!" the girl who rung me up said.

"I just did!" I replied.

Just as I said that, I realized the price tag for the jeans under my sweats was poking out. I booked it out the door, with the security hot on my heels. I assumed he'd stop chasing me once I got far, but he didn't. He was pretty fast, and I was scared as hell. As I was running, that same Lexus from about a week ago pulled up. The passenger window rolled down, and I saw Julius alone.

"Who you running from? Get in!" he yelled. I didn't hesitate, and pulled on his door handle. He sped off, and I saw the security guy stop to catch his breath.

"Fuck," I said as I plopped my head on the headrest.

"What the hell, ma?! What you running from?" Julius chuckled as he drove.

"Fucking security, at bitch ass Oscar's!" I spat, as if they had stolen from me.

"You ain't out here stealing, is you?" he asked.

"I am," I inhaled, and his cologne invaded my nostrils.

"You too pretty for that."

"No such thing," I replied, looking out the window.

He chuckled. "So this is how you spend your Sunday nights?" he smiled.

"Ain't shit else for a 16 year old to do," I spat.

"Want to come party with the homies?" he asked.

I didn't want to seem like a square and say no. I wasn't no fucking square, by the way.

"I can fuck with it for a bit," I replied, trying to sound cool although I was nervous.

Julius chuckled and picked up his speed. We arrived to a nice-sized house, and I wondered if this was his own.

"Your momma let you have parties?" I asked, unbuckling my seat belt.

"I don't live with my momma, shorty," Julius replied. He smiled, and he had the most alluring smile ever. He was sucking on a jolly rancher candy, and he made it look so good. I had never seen a guy as sexy as him that wasn't on TV.

We exited the car and as we got closer, I heard "Bitches N Marijuana" by Chris Brown and Tyga bumping. Julius opened his door, and I followed him in. It was about seven people there, including Bianca and that ass-wipe from my job.

"The stuck up hoe from CVS!" the ass-wipe smiled.

"Fuck you," I spat, making everyone laugh.

"She on you, Greg!" some random laughed.

"Have a seat," Bianca smiled, and patted the couch pillow next to her.

I felt so under dressed. All these chicks in here had on expensive brands, and I didn't. I had on those sweats, my usual knock off Keds, and a burgundy shirt. My long, chestnut-colored hair was down with a part down the middle. Julius came and sat next to me, so now I was sandwiched between he and his girlfriend.

"You want a drink, Natalia?" Bianca stood up.

"She 16, ma," Julius said.

"Who waits until they're 21 anymore?" Bianca chuckled.

"How old are you?" I asked Julius, raising my brow.

"19," he replied.

"Oh," I said, caught off guard. I thought he was my age.

My phone buzzed, and I pulled it out to see Frank's name. "That's your nigga?" Julius asked.

"No. Hell no!" I replied, frowning.

"Just a fuck buddy?" he smiled, hypnotizing me again. His peanut butter skin was flawless, and his lips looked so soft.

"I don't fuck," I replied.

"You a virgin?" he asked surprised, and I nodded.

"Natalia, what are you? Part Russian or some shit?" Greg asked.

"No, I don't know," I shrugged.

"How the fuck you don't know?" Greg shook his head and laughed. I hated his ass, and this was only the second time I was around him.

"Cause my momma don't know what all she is, and she only told me my daddy was black. So maybe I'm mixed, maybe I ain't nigga," I spat, and everyone laughed.

"Little spicy 16 year old!" someone said. There were thick clouds of smoke, so I couldn't see whom.

"You smoke?" Bianca asked, returning with my drink. I nodded and sipped it. It was cranberry and vodka; my favorite. Bianca lit up a blunt, and then passed it to me.

I smoked and drank all damn night, until the wee hours of the morning. I woke up on the couch, and saw it was 9 a.m. *Fuck.* School started at 8:15. I grabbed my phone, and saw I had five missed calls from Lucy.

"Good morning, sleepy head," Bianca smiled, walking out with just a wife beater on. She had way more body than I'd ever seen, just like my mother.

"Good morning. Do you think I can get a ride to school?" I asked squinting. My head was killing me.

"I ain't dressed, but Julius can," she pointed over her shoulder.

"Come on ma," Julius said, entering the room. He looked so sexy in a gray pullover, dark jeans, and gray low top chucks. He wore a gray snapback to complete the look. His cologne smelled so good, and temporarily relieved my headache.

"You gon' go to school without washing ya ass?" Bianca frowned up.

"No," I said, plopping back down on the couch. I had enough problems; I was not going to school in cheap clothes *and* un-bathed.

***

"Who you live with?" Julius asked as he drove me home. "My sister," I lied. Shit, Dalia *was* more of a sister than a mom.

"Cool," he nodded as he pulled up to my apartment complex. "Let me get your number, Natalia." Julius said as he parked the car.

"You ha-have a girlfriend," I replied, looking into his perfect face.

"We friends, ain't we? I just want to make sure you good on occasions. It ain't nothing like what you think," he smiled, and so did I.

I read off my number, and he stored it. My phone chimed, and I looked at the screen hoping it wasn't Frank's thirsty ass. I saw it was an un-stored number.

"That's me," Julius said.

"K. Thanks for the ride," I replied, and hopped out quickly.

I couldn't wait to tell Lucy about me turning up with Julius and his friends all night.

It was Friday night, and I was happy I didn't work tomorrow. I was laying in bed after a nice hot shower, when I heard my phone play "Lady in a Glass Dress" by Chris Brown. It was around 1 a.m., so I knew it was probably Frank. As soon as I found out how to block him, I would. I decided to check it so it wouldn't notify me again, and saw it was Julius. A smile crept across my face, but it faded once I thought of Bianca. I slid open my iPhone, and clicked my messages app.

Julius: Natalia! Are you part Russian?

Me: No! Lol.

Julius: Ohhhh lol. Wyd?

Me: Watching TV.

Julius: Come outside.

Me: Okay.

I didn't know why he was here, but I was bored. I threw on a white t-shirt, some grey velour shorts, and flip-flops. I unwrapped my long hair, which was now pressed, and let it cascade down my back. I grabbed my house keys and phone, and then ran through the apartment.

"Where you going Natalia?" my mother asked.

"Just to see a friend downstairs," I replied.

She looked me up and down suspiciously. "Don't be opening your legs, Natalia!" she spat, and went back to her room. It's not like she cared; she just didn't want me getting pregnant cause she didn't want any babies around.

I ran down my steps, and out the complex gate. I spotted Julius' Lexus and headed over. I heard him unlock the doors, so I tugged on the handle.

"Hi," I said as I got in. His cologne smelled heavenly, and it mixed nicely with the coconut air freshener. I could see his eyes were low under his red snapback, so I knew he was high. He was sucking on a jolly rancher again, looking so sexy.

"Sup ma," he looked over at me and smiled. His full lips against his peanut butter skin made me feel hot all over. *What was he doing to me?*

"So this how you spend your Friday nights?" I asked, using his words against him.

"In the company of beautiful girls? All the time," he winked.

"Where is Bianca?" I asked, feeling nervous.

"At work," he replied.

"Work? Where does she work this late?" I asked. I knew she didn't work at a pharmacy like me.

"Strip club," Julius chuckled.

"Oh," I replied.

"Let's go to the crib," he said as he cranked up his car and pulled off. I wanted to protest, but I didn't.

We arrived to his house, and hopped out immediately. Once we entered, I noticed the house was much cleaner than last time. I actually got to see the house with a clear head.

"Cleaned up?" I said as I sat down.

"Nah, Bianca did," he replied, walking to his kitchen.

"Thirsty?" he asked.

"Yes," I replied. He returned from the kitchen with some Smirnoff Ice drinks.

"Thank you," I said as he sat down.

We decided to watch Boardwalk Empire on HBO Go. I was disappointed at first, cause I didn't like those types of shows, but it was pretty interesting. After watching a couple episodes, Julius draped his arm around me, and I froze up.

"What would Bianca say if she knew I was here, alone with you?" I asked nervously.

"She won't know," he replied. He leaned down, and started to kiss on my neck.

"Julius…" I moaned.

He reached his hand between my legs, and began to massage my pussy through my velour shorts. It was feeling good as hell, and I was wondering why. He kissed up my face, and then my lips. His full lips against my full lips felt like heaven on Earth. He switched back and forth between sucking my top lip, and sucking my bottom lip, and it felt so good that I forgot where I was for a moment.

"Julius wait, I can't do this. I don't want to," I said. He kissed my cheek, and then my lips again.

"I ain't never kissed another girl on the lips while with Bianca. I just bust my nut and dip. For some reason, I really want to fuck with you, Natalia," he said as he planted soft kisses on my lips. Butterflies consumed my stomach as I closed my eyes and let him make love to my mouth. I could taste the blue raspberry jolly rancher he ate a couple hours ago, mixed with the watermelon Smirnoff.

"Can you take me home?" I said, breaking away from his kiss.

"Why?" he asked, biting his plump, bottom lip. I needed to get out of here, because I was liking what he did. I didn't want to lose my virginity to someone who was involved, especially when I knew his girlfriend.

"Cause I don't want to do this," I said in a low tone. I prayed that he complied.

He stared into my eyes for a little bit, then pecked me once more.

"Aight, come on," he finally said, getting off the couch.

On the way to my house, he didn't say a word to me. We just listened to Kendrick Lamar the whole time. After about 15 minutes, we finally arrived at my house.

"Are you mad at me?" I asked, placing my hand on the seat belt release button.

"Not mad at all," he smiled and bit his lip, hypnotizing me.

"Okay, good. Goodnight," I smiled, and got out the car.

I ran up the stairs and texted Lucy all the details. I couldn't talk to Julius anymore.

Don't get it twisted now; I liked Bianca a lot, but Natalia's young ass was sexy as fuck. When I first saw her at CVS, I knew I wanted to fuck. I was kind of upset that she was 16, but that didn't stop me from thinking about banging her out 24/7. Her smooth caramel complexion was mouth watering. I loved her long brown hair, nice little fat ass, small perky breasts, and smooth toned thighs. She wasn't as thick as the girls I'm used to smashing, but she was just as bad nonetheless. I knew I had a problem when I kissed her lips. I've fucked a lot of hoes on the side, but made sure to keep my lips to myself. Natalia was different though; I knew I wanted to fuck her on more than one occasion.

Anyway, my name is Julius Tate, and you guessed it - I'm a hustler. I sell dope and I make good money doing so. I tried other jobs and shit, but they never worked out for me. I was always either late, missing days, or taking a break for too damn long. I wasn't tripping though, because the lifestyle I wanted, those jobs couldn't afford. The type of money I bring in at the moment allows me to afford a nice small house, my Lexus, and nice clothes and jewelry. That's all I really need, because the hoes came even when I was broke as fuck. At the moment, I work for someone else's operation, but I have plans in the works to have my own shit running. My mother named me after the most famous Roman dictator, Julius Caesar, and it was a perfect fit for me because I was born to run shit, not follow along. I ain't gon' come up out here in Indiana though, because I ain't one to step on toes, especially the toes of a nigga who put me on.

I worked for a nigga named Hugo, and he was rich as hell. He ran a tight fucking ship, but that only meant constant bread. You never had to wonder if you was getting good money, cause it was a no brainer. Hugo found me when I was robbing niggas, and decided to put me on. He said I had heart, and treated me like a son. Shit, a nigga didn't have a father, so it felt good to have that bond with somebody. My mother was a crack head, and we really didn't fuck with each other. Her bad ass habit was the reason we were on the streets and shit. Being a stick up kid was the only way I knew to make money. That was another reason I liked Natalia; she was a hustler. She didn't have the means, but instead of sitting on her ass looking for a rich nigga to take care of her, she went out and got it; that shit turned me on lowkey.

Bianca was a hustler, sort of. As long as she could strip, she could make money but if she couldn't strip, she'd be broke. The club she worked at, Black Light, was a pretty popping ass spot, so she made a good amount. However, Bianca blew her money on labels, and lived paycheck-to-paycheck pretty much. That doesn't really apply to strippers per say, but you know what I mean. Soon as she blew her money, she was in my face with her fucking hand out. She had no goals outside of the strip club, and that shit was a turn off.

"I'm hungry babe," Bianca whined.

"What you got a taste for, ma?" I asked.

"St. Elmo's," she smiled.

"Come on," I replied, shaking my head.

I was starting to feel like a fucking sugar daddy. I didn't mind spending money on my lady, but I didn't feel Bianca deserved it. Our relationship just kind of happened. She was a good ass fuck buddy, and then just kind of maneuvered her way into my life. I wasn't tripping, because I still smashed other hoes whenever I wanted; she knew that too.

"Is that Natalia?" I said out loud as we drove down the street.

"Oh yeah. It is," Bianca nodded. "What are you doing?" she asked when she saw me slowing down.

I rolled down Bianca's window, "Hey ma," I smiled.

"Oh, hey Julius. Hi Bianca," Natalia half smiled. I wanted to get in her ass about ignoring my texts for the past three weeks, but I couldn't in front of Bianca.

"Where you headed?" I asked.

"To my best friend Lucy's house," she smiled, avoiding eye contact. Damn she was so beautiful. Maybe it wasn't good for me to fuck with her, cause I was not tryna fall in love. A nigga like me couldn't love any bitches, cause of my weak ass mama.

"You want a ride?" I asked, and Bianca looked at me.

"No, I'm almost there," she replied.

"Get in Natalia," I said, ignoring her protest. She did as I asked, and I drove her to Lucy's.

"Thank you, Julius. Bye Bianca," Natalia said as she hopped out. I watched her as she walked up the porch steps of her friend's house.

"You like that little bitch, don't you?" Bianca asked, shaking her head.

"What? Hell nah!" I frowned.

"You text her all fucking day, and every time you see her you giving her a ride!" Bianca spat.

"Who the fuck you yelling at, Bianca?!" I frowned.

"I'm sorry, Julius," she replied and paused. "It's just, I love you and I don't want you interested in nobody else," she pouted.

"Ain't nobody interested in Natalia's little ass, aight?" I said, agitated.

NATALIA

THREE WEEKS LATER

Although I had a job, my checks weren't big enough. I was still shopping at hand-me-down stores, and stores that had $5.99 in the name. I was still going to sleep hungry as hell some nights. I checked the fridge and slammed it, cause nothing was in it but a bottle of wine, and my mother was gone out as usual. I gave up and headed back to my room. It was Saturday night, and I was on the phone with Lucy.

"You let Julius fuck you yet?" Lucy laughed.

"Hell no, I told you it ain't gon' happen," I smiled as I twirled my hair around my finger.

"But you said you liked what he did to you that night. Annndd y'all talk all day and night!" Lucy said.

"Yeah, but that don't mean I'm gon' fuck someone else's boyfriend!" I frowned.

"He sounds more like your boyfriend than hers. Plus, it'd just be one time," she laughed.

"You think I'm gon' give my virginity up for a one night stand? You really are a hoe," I chuckled.

"Maybe I am. Oh, thank you for that money by the way," she said.

"No problem, you know I- hold on. I'm getting another call," I said, hearing my phone beep. I pulled it from my face, and saw Julius' name. He got in my ass about ignoring him a couple weeks back, so ever since then we talked constantly. "Hello," I tried to hold in my smile.

"What you doing beautiful?" he asked. I loved hearing him call me that, but I couldn't get sucked in.

"On the phone with my best friend," I smiled as if he could see.

"Let's go eat. You hungry?"

"Yeah," I replied. "Wait, what about Bianca?" I asked.

"Stop asking questions like that, aight?" he said sternly.

"Okay," I replied.

"I'm gon' be at your house in a minute, don't keep me waiting," he said.

"Okay," I replied.

I disconnected with him, and picked back up with Lucy. I let her know I was tired, and gonna go to bed. I didn't want her to know the truth, because I knew she would be all in my ear about fucking Julius. *I wasn't gon' fuck him! Damn!* I dug through my cheap ass wardrobe, and settled on a dark blue dress. I wasn't sure what material it was, but it was thin. I slid into my flip-flops, and let my curly brown hair hang. I grabbed my last $10 bucks, and prayed we went to IHOP or something cheap.

"Hey," I said as I got in.

"You look beautiful. Gimme a kiss," Julius said, staring deeply into my eyes.

"Julius I can't-"

"Give me a kiss," he repeated, cutting me off. I leaned over and planted a kiss on his lips. He dipped his tongue in my mouth as I cupped his face. "You gon' be mine. You know that, right?" he said in between kisses. I pulled away, and put on my seat belt. He chuckled and pulled off.

I saw we arrived to Olive Garden, which was not in my budget.

"I can't afford Olive Garden, Julius," I said.

"I got you ma," he smiled, and kissed my lips again. He got out, then came around to open my door.

We walked to the restaurant hand in hand, and he opened the door for me. I couldn't lie; it felt good to be on Julius' arm like this. The hostess seated us, and let us know the waitress would be over to us soon.

"Hello, my name is Kina. I'm gonna be your waitress today," the waitress smiled. She stared at Julius lustfully, and I was actually jealous.

"Baby, you go ahead first," Julius said.

I smiled at him calling me that, until I thought of Bianca. "Can I have water please?" I said.

"I thought you said you liked strawberry lemonade?" Julius frowned. *He remembered.*

"I know but it's $4," I replied.

"It's good, ma. She will have the strawberry lemonade, and I will take a regular lemonade," he said.

"Okay, I will be back with those shortly," she said, licking her lips. I didn't like her ass.

"Why did you call me baby?" I asked once the waitress left.

"Cause you my baby." He flashed his perfect smile. His features were so perfect, from his peanut butter complexion, to his small nose and plump lips. "Don't you wanna be my baby?" he asked me, while I was being captivated by his features. He took my small hands into his, and I admired his strong grip; I felt safe.

"Yeah, but I can't," I said in a low tone.

"Why?" he asked.

"Cause you're taken," I replied.

"Nah, we are broken up Natalia," he said, licking his lips. The way he said my name sent chills down my spine.

"You-you are?" I stuttered.

"Yeah," he smirked, and kissed the back of my hand.

After we finished dinner, we headed to his house. I was scared as hell to be alone with him, knowing he and Bianca were no longer. We walked in, and he immediately led me to his bedroom. He turned on a simple nightlight, giving the room a little bit of illumination. I stood there not knowing what to do, as I admired his nice bedroom. It was large, with a hug bed, a plasma TV, two big dressers, a closet with mirror doors, and a bathroom on the left side. He closed the door, then walked closer to me. I backed up a little, scared of what was to come. He towered over me, and dipped his tongue in my mouth. I decided not to fight him anymore, and let my body enjoy his kisses.

"You gonna let me make love to you?" he whispered as he kissed my neck, and raised my dress.

"Julius...I'm-"

"Don't be scared, Natalia," he whispered as he pulled my dress up.

Once my dress was off, he stepped back to admire my body. He removed his shirt, and continued to stare at my body. "You're so beautiful," he whispered, as his eyes roamed my physique.

"Sorry, I don't have nice sets," I said, referring to my undergarments. I had on some cheap plaid panty and bra set that cost me $4 on sale.

"Shhhh, you're perfect," he said as he neared me. He towered over me, grabbed my face, and kissed me passionately.

"I love you Julius," I said in between kisses.

He smiled and unhooked my bra. He placed me on the bed, and climbed on top of me in just his boxers. I felt his dick pressing against my vagina, and it felt big. He kissed from my lips to my neck, then to my nipples, which he devoured.

"Ahhh," I moaned, and arched my back.

He reached his hand down into my panties, and played with my clit. I realized I was wet, and became embarrassed as fuck.

"Mmmm," he moaned as he sucked my nipples. The more he did that, the wetter I became. "You so wet baby," Julius commented.

"I'm sorry," I replied embarrassed.

"Nah, that's a good thing ma. The wetter the better," he replied smiling.

He tugged my panties down and kissed my stomach softly, sending chills up my spine. He stood on his knees to release his dick, and it was the biggest thing I had ever seen. It looked to be about 11 inches, and I became scared.

"Wait, Julius," I said, scared to death.

He lowered himself back between my legs, letting his dick lie against my bare vagina. "You wanna be my girl?" he asked as he kissed my lips softly and constantly. I nodded and wrapped my arms around his neck. "Then you got to be able to please me. If you can't, I got to get it from somewhere else," he said, looking into my eyes. I nodded to say I understood. He smiled and placed my legs over his biceps.

"Wait, a condom," I said. He ignored me and dipped his tongue in my mouth.

I felt his thick head at my opening, and I shut my eyes to prepare for the worst. "Open your eyes," he said as he kissed me passionately. "I want you to look me in the eyes the whole time," he said, and I nodded.

"Ahhh, ahhh, Julius!" I yelped as he entered me inch by inch. He spread my legs some more to be able to fit fully. "Slow down," I whined.

"Damn ma, this is so good," he moaned as he sucked my lips. "This may be the best pussy yet," he moaned. "Fuck," he said as he sped up a little.

"Ahhh. Ahh," I moaned as he tore into me. He kissed me some more, to help ease my mind.

"This is my pussy now, Natalia. You hear me?" he asked as he thrusted into me in a slow, circular motion.

"Yessss," I moaned as I felt myself release liquid on his dick. My body jerked, and Julius smiled.

"That's right, cum on this dick baby," he moaned as he sped up. He pinned my hands above my head and started fucking me real fast. He finally released a warm liquid into my body, and pressed his lips against mine.

"The only nigga you open your legs for is me," he said in between kisses.

"Okay. I love you," I replied as he sucked my lips and chin.

He pulled out of me, flipped me over, and entered me from behind. He fucked me all night, until 4 in the morning. I was just happy to know I lost my virginity to the man I loved.

"You sure this ain't too tight?" I asked Lucy as I looked in my full-length mirror. It was a burgundy, sleeveless, turtleneck dress, which stopped a couple inches above my knee.

"No you look super cute," she smiled as she put some more gloss on. She wore booty shorts, and a tube top. Her fair skin was blemish free, and her shoulder length hair was bone straight. Lucy was the lightest black person I had ever seen.

We were going to a party that some guy named Menzo was having. Lucy and him had fucked around a bit, so he invited her. She let me know ahead of time that we may be the youngest girls there.

"We ready, Dalia," I told my mother. She made me pay her $6 for a ride two blocks away. I didn't mind walking, but Lucy wore heels so she did. I had on some cute sandals, cause heels weren't my thing.

"Dinero please," she said, holding her hand out. I placed the six ones in her hand, and grabbed my phone and house keys.

My phone buzzed on the way there, and I saw it was a text from Julius.

Boyfriend: *Come straight to my crib when you wake up tomorrow.*

. . .

Me: *Okay.*

Boyfriend: *You love me?*

Me: *Yes.*

Boyfriend: *Tell me.*

Me: *I love you Julius.*

Boyfriend: *Good girl.*

After about ten minutes, my mom pulled up at the address Lucy gave her. We hopped out, and I winced in pain.

"You let him fuck!" Lucy bucked her eyes and smiled.

"No I didn't," I said, pushing my hair behind my ears.

"Why are you so sore?" she raised a brow.

"Fine," I smiled

"I knew he was gonna break you down!" she laughed as we walked up the walkway.

"He's my man now though," I smiled.

The music was loud as hell, and Lucy and I started to dance as we reached the door. "Face Down" by Lil Boosie was the current song, and I couldn't wait to let loose. Once we got inside, we saw the party was lit up with purple lights, and everybody was getting they freak on. I'm talking lap dances, floor grinding, and all kinds of shit. Lucy and I decided to head to the punch bowl and make ourselves a drink to get started.

"Natalia!"

I looked over to see Bianca smiling. My heart dropped when I saw she was sitting in Julius' lap. Lucy looked at me and shook her head. I took some deep breaths to hold back the tears as we made our way over.

"What you doing here?" Julius smiled as he held Bianca's waist tightly.

I couldn't hold it in anymore, so I rushed to the bathroom. I closed the door and plopped down on the toilet top. I cried hard, not caring who could hear outside the door. I was so stupid to have sex with Julius. I should've known he only wanted one thing from me. The worst part was that I was still in love.

JULIUS

I was not expecting Natalia to be at my boy Menzo's party. I was caught off guard when I heard Bianca call her name. I saw the hurt in her eyes as she looked at us. Originally, I was just trying to hit and quit. Unfortunately, I realized I enjoyed spending time with her prior to fucking her. I had feelings for this young bitch, and a part of me felt like a fucking weak ass nigga.

I tried to ignore her running off, but I couldn't. I moved Bianca off my lap after waiting a couple minutes, so it wouldn't look suspicious. I rushed to the back, and heard Natalia crying behind the bathroom door. I knocked lightly after seeing the door was locked.

"I'll be ou-out in a minute," she stuttered through tears.

"It's me baby," I said, and looked over my shoulder to make sure Bianca was nowhere in sight.

"I'm not your baby," she cried.

"Yes you are. Let me in," I replied.

It was quiet for a little bit, and then she unlocked the door. I twisted the knob and walked in, then locked the door. She looked so beautiful, even with tears drenching her face. I hated that I wanted her ass. I didn't want to have feelings for no bitch, especially not a 16-year-old.

"Why did you use me, Julius?" she cried.

"Come here. I didn't use you," I said, pulling her into a hug. I sat her up on the wide sink, and positioned myself between her legs. I grabbed her face, and dipped my tongue in her mouth.

"I loved you Julius," she said in a low tone, as I tongued her down.

I turned my snapback backwards, since it was in the way. She grabbed onto my pullover as we got lost in our kiss.

"You don't love me no more?" I asked, kissing her soft neck. Her perfume smelled so sweet. I rubbed my hands up her dress, and squeezed her smooth ass.

"I still love you," she replied. "What about Bianca?" she asked as I moved her panties to the side.

"What I tell you about those questions? You my girl and that's all you need to know," I told her. Natalia wasn't my girl, but I was gon' try to handle her and Bianca at the same time. Honestly, Natalia was who I wanted, but I couldn't end my relationship with someone my age for a 16-year-old. As much as I wanted to believe I wanted Bianca over Natalia, I knew it wasn't true. Natalia was simple, and I loved that shit. She didn't need the glitz and glam, and she didn't try to keep up with the Jones'.

I released my pole, and wiggled my way into her tight pussy.

"Fuck," I moaned. I lifted her small frame, and brought her up and down on my dick slowly. "Hollywood Dreams" by Miguel blasted over the party, and it went perfectly with our impromptu lovemaking.

"Ahhh. Ahhh," Natalia moaned in my mouth as she came.

I sped up some, and finally released into her. I needed to stop fucking this girl raw, but I couldn't help it. I wanted to be one with her sexy ass. I kissed her soft lips, letting my dick sit inside her. I finally slid out slow, and wiped my dick off with a wet paper towel. She did the same with her pussy, and then I towered over her to kiss her lips.

"I'm gon' get rid of Bianca ASAP," I lied, hugging her from behind.

"Don't call until you do," she said, and walked towards the door.

I grabbed her arm, and turned her to face me. I rushed her into the wall, and kissed her lips. "How did you get me here, ma?" I said as I kissed her lips. She smiled, flashing her pretty teeth. "Don't dance with no niggas," I warned her before she left.

"I won't," she said, as she left the bathroom.

I waited a couple minutes, and walked out after her.

"Where you was at?" Bianca frowned once I walked up.

"Phone call," I said, keeping my eyes locked on Natalia. This little girl was about to fuck my life up, and she didn't even know it.

"I don't want you hanging out with Natalia anymore," Bianca said as we slept with our backs to one another.

"Too bad," I replied.

"I'm serious Julius! I know you like her, you pervert!" she yelled.

I rolled over, grabbed her neck, and squeezed. "Watch your damn mouth, bitch," I said through gritted teeth. I watched her claw at my hands for a bit before letting her go. "Get out my damn bed and go home!" I yelled, not wanting her near me.

"Julius, it's 3 a.m.," she whined.

"Go!" I yelled loud as hell.

She pushed me, and then proceeded to get out the bed. I grabbed her by her hair. "Quit playing with me Bianca," I said.

"Arrgghhh," she groaned as I held her hair tightly. I let her go, and she immediately grabbed her scalp. "I love you Julius! How could you even do me like this?" she cried.

"Have I ever said I loved you back?" I asked.

She paused, and then grabbed her stuff. I heard her sniffling, and then she left.

I loved Julius with all my heart. I knew he fucked around with different bitches, but I was always the main. I didn't trip that he got his dick wet with other bitches every now and then, because I knew I was the only one that mattered.

Natalia was different though, and I didn't like it. I saw the way he looked at her when we first met her at CVS, and it definitely gave me an uneasy feeling. I decided to ignore it, because I knew Julius would just fuck her and keep it pushing.

Unfortunately, that wasn't the case at all. He would rush out every morning to go drive Natalia and her best friend to school, and then he would pick her up too. He would constantly text her while we hung out together, and would sneak away to talk with her on the phone. His daily routine had become: take Natalia to school, work the streets, pick her up from school, back to working the streets, come home and talk to her.

I hated that I worked most nights, because I knew he was smashing her in my bed; well, his bed that we shared when I slept over. I hated her ass, because we were supposed to be friends, yet she was fucking my man.

"Julius up in here," my best friend Daphne pointed out to me. We both worked at Black Light Gentleman's club.

"Where?" I asked, frantically scanning the room.

"VIP," she pointed.

I looked over and spotted Julius with this stripper named Queen in his lap. He was feeling her up as she grinded her ass on him. They were violating the no touching policy like a muthafucka. This, in combination with treating Natalia like she was his main bitch, had me hot. I stormed over there to confront this nigga; I was tired of the games.

"Really Julius?!" I frowned, pushing Queen out of his lap.

"Damn Allure!" Queen yelled, calling me by my stage name. She stormed off, sipping on a drink.

"I told you when you come here to only get dances from me!" I yelled at Julius.

"You don't tell me what the fuck to do, Bianca!" he spat, and his friends shook their heads.

"So all you care about is that bitch now?" I asked.

"What bitch?" he frowned.

"Natalia!" I spat.

"Man, I done told you I ain't fucking with that girl," he replied frowning.

"Yeah you better not be!" I yelled. "Ah!" I yelped as he grabbed my hand. He squeezed it tight, almost breaking my fingers.

"What I tell you about your fucking mouth, hunh? Don't make me beat yo ass in front of all these people bitch," he said in a low tone, as tears from the pain escaped my eyes.

"Okay, okay. I'm sorry Julius," I whimpered. He gave my hand one more squeeze, then threw it.

"Get out my fucking way!" he said storming out, along with Greg, this dude named Dash, and Menzo.

I ran to the back to get dressed, so I could follow him. I didn't want him running up behind Natalia's young ass, just cause he was mad at me. Once dressed, I ran out to the parking lot, where I saw he was gone already. I sped to his house, hoping he was there alone. Fifteen minutes later I was pulling up, and I breathed a sigh of relief when I saw his car parked there. I rested my head against the headrest as I inspected my hand.

After about 15 minutes of just thinking and shit, I exited the car. I knocked on the door, and no one answered. I knocked a couple more times, and still got nothing. I pulled out my cell and called Julius about three times, and got no answer each time. I was about to walk away, but I heard a female laughing and it sounded like Queen. I stepped to the side once I heard the door being unlocked. Out walked Queen as I expected, and her eyes bucked when she saw me.

"Bitch you fucked my nigga?" I yelled, and grabbed her by the hair.

I slung her down off the porch, and she fell to the ground. I climbed on top of her, and started delivering blows to her face. After a couple punches, I felt myself being lifted off of her and carried away.

"What the fuck is wrong with you?!" Julius yelled, sitting me down.

"Stupid bitch! Ain't my fault your pussy is wack!" Queen yelled.

Julius stormed over to her and grabbed her by the hand. They headed back inside, and I charged them both. I ran dead smack into the screen door, and then Julius came back out alone.

"Go home Bianca," Julius said, standing in his front doorway.

"Go home? You seriously about to have this bitch spend the night with you?!" I frowned in disbelief.

"Maybe. Now get the fuck away from over here, causing all this fucking ruckus!" Julius frowned. He had his shirt off, with jeans on that were unzipped, so I knew he fucked her already.

I admired his sexy body and beautiful face. His caramel complexion was adorned with tattoos, covering most of his 6-foot frame. His sexy face was chiseled to perfection, and his full lips made me wet on sight. I dropped my head defeated, and walked back to my car. I checked my phone all night, and never once received a text or call from his ass.

"What are you doing here?" I asked Julius as I walked in my bedroom.

I was fresh from the shower and wrapped in a towel. He stood up off my bed, and pulled my towel from me. "Oh now you want me after kicking me out last night?" I frowned.

"Yep," he simply replied.

He removed his shirt, and I walked over to unbuckle his pants. I released his dick, and dropped to my knees. I made it disappear, and drenched it with my saliva as I bobbed up and down. I massaged his balls as he fucked my face.

"Damn, Bianca. Fuck," Julius moaned as my pussy got wetter from the sound of my name on his lips.

He busted down my throat, and then I laid back on the bed. I spread my legs wide, giving him full view of my bald kitten. "Why don't you try it?" I asked, biting my lip.

"You know I don't do that," he replied, and flipped me over.

Julius said he didn't eat pussy, but we all knew what that meant. Julius just didn't want to eat *my* pussy. Anytime a person says they don't give head, it means you just ain't the person they want to give head to; you ain't brought that out of them.

"Oooh damn," I felt Julius slide inside me after putting a condom on. I loved that Julius never fucked raw, which is why him smashing these other hoes didn't bother me as much; he was being safe.

He plowed into me, beating my pussy up. He constantly hit my spot, making me cum three times. He grabbed a handful of my weave, and went full speed ahead.

"Uhhhh, Uhhhhh, fuck!" I moaned as we exploded together.

He smacked me on the ass, and then went to flush the condom. I grabbed my towel, and went to follow him.

"I was thinking we could go have breakfast together," I said.

"Nah, I gotta shower, then go meet with Hugo," he replied.

"You don't ever make time for me anymore, Julius," I whined.

"I just did, but I got you later tonight," he said, and kissed my cheek.

"No lip?" I frowned.

He didn't respond, as he dipped out the door.

It was Friday, and I was so damn tired leaving work. The only thing that got me through my shift was the fact that I didn't work tomorrow.

Julius had been on my mind constantly. He hadn't talked to me since our bathroom encounter, which was weeks ago. I was so damn depressed, and feeling dumber than ever.

I pulled out my phone, and decided to call him. It rang and rang, and I got no answer as usual. A couple tears managed to cascade down my cheeks, as my phone buzzed. I quickly wiped them and smiled. I saw Frank was calling, and immediately frowned.

"Hey," I said answering.

"What you doing tomorrow?" Frank asked.

"Probably nothing," I said, looking around and making sure no one was running up on me.

"Let's go see a movie," Frank replied.

"Frank-"

"Come on ma, I been chasing you for months," he pleaded.

I paused for a second, as I walked up my apartment steps.

"Okay," I finally said, and disconnected.

Once in the house, I checked my phone and saw I had no messages from Julius. I shook my head, and then proceeded to shower. I washed my body with my Herbal Essence body wash, braided my long hair, and then dozed off.

"You want to go eat?" Frank asked me as he drove from the theatre.

"Not really," I replied. Ever since Julius cut me off, I hadn't had an appetite.

"Aight well I guess I can take you home," he replied.

I didn't respond, and just hoped he sped there. He pulled up to my house, and shut the engine off as if he wasn't about to leave.

"Well thanks for the movie, Frank," I said as I grabbed my jacket from his back seat.

"Damn, we can't chill for a bit?" he chuckled.

"Okay," I said.

"I really like you, Natalia," he said, rubbing my thigh. He leaned over and started placing kisses on my neck.

"Frank do-"

"Come on ma," he said in a low tone. He was fine as hell, but I just wasn't in the mood to fuck someone else already. He kissed my lips, and dipped his tongue in my mouth. Just as he glided his hands up to my vagina, the passenger door flung open. We both jumped and I saw it was Julius, with wrath written all over his face.

"Aye man what the fuck!" Frank yelled.

"Shut yo ass up before I shut you up for good," Julius frowned.

Frank did as he was told, and Julius snatched me out the car by my arm. He pulled me into my complex, and up to my door. "Unlock it!" he yelled. I did as I was told, and he pushed me in. "What the fuck did I tell you?!" he spat, slamming the door. This was the only time I wished my mother was home.

"I- I don't rememb-"

"Oh you don't? So you let this nigga fuck?" he frowned and slapped me across the face. My lip split, and blood gushed from it.

"Wait, no Julius I didn-" I tried to say, but he cut me off with another slap to the face.

"You can't hit me!" I yelled through tears. I ran away to my room and slammed the door shut. I locked it, and then looked in the mirror at my face. I'd seen women get beat up in the movies, and I couldn't believe it was happening to me.

"Open the fucking door!" Julius yelled, beating on it hard.

"Please leave Julius!" I cried. There was silence for a bit, but I didn't hear the front door open so I knew he was still here.

"Baby, I'm sorry. Open the door," he said in a calmer tone.

I didn't respond as I sat in my closet, scared as hell. Blood was dripping from my nose onto my forearms, as I sat in the fetal position. The next thing I knew, I heard my bedroom door being busted through. My closet door flew open, and Julius snatched me up out the closet. He pulled me close and hugged me tight.

"I'm sorry baby. I just don't want you fucking around," he said as I sniffled.

"I-I di-didn't sle-sleep wi-with hi-him, Julius," I stuttered through tears.

"Get some stuff, we leaving," he replied.

He let me go, and I started to pack a bag. I was scared to leave with him, but too scared to protest his wishes. Once I packed an outfit, I went to the bathroom to clean my face.

"Brush your fucking teeth. I saw that nigga's tongue all in your mouth," Julius spat as he stood in the doorway of the bathroom. He wore gray sweats, a white t-shirt with black writing on it, white socks, and black Jordan slide ins.

I brushed my teeth, and then we headed out the door. It was about 8 p.m. sharp, so it was dark outside when we pulled up to the house. We walked inside, and headed to the bedroom. As soon as we got in there, Julius shoved his tongue in my mouth. He undressed me down to just my underwear, and laid me down.

"Why haven't you called?" I asked as he kissed down my stomach. He didn't say anything as he tugged my panties down. He placed my thighs on his shoulders, and took my clit into his mouth. He told me he didn't do this, so I was caught off guard. He sucked my clit, and dipped his tongue in my hole.

"Ahh, I missed you so much Julius," I moaned as he made me cum. He pushed my legs back towards me, and dove in again. "Ahhh Ahhh," I moaned as I came again. He licked up all my juices, and then kissed back up my body.

"Oh my God!"

I heard a voice say. I looked in the doorway, and there stood Bianca. She charged towards us, and Julius hopped up to block her.

"How the fuck you get in my crib?!" he barked.

"For real Julius? I thought you said you didn't like her!" she yelled, hurting my feelings. I covered my exposed body with the sheet.

"Get the fuck out, Bianca!" Julius yelled, shoving her towards the door.

"I'm gon' fuck you up, bitch!" Bianca yelled to me, as Julius pushed her outside.

I heard them arguing some more, so I got up to get dressed. I was hurt by what Julius told Bianca.

"Where you going?" Julius asked, walking back in.

"Home," I replied.

"No you not, he said, grabbing me and kissing me hard.

He took my panties back off, and laid me back down. He climbed between my legs, and dipped his tongue in my mouth again.

"Did you really tell Bianca you didn't like me?" I asked as I felt the head of his dick at my opening.

"Nah, she just mad cause you my girl now," he replied, making me smile.

"Uhhh, ahhhh," I moaned as he entered me fully. "This still hurts Julius," I whined.

"Relax, Natalia. Shit you feel good," he moaned as he thrusted into me.

"I love you, Julius," I moaned as he dipped his tongue in my mouth.

He continued to thrust into me slowly, as he pinned my hands above my head. He sped up his pace and the sound of how wet I was, mixed with our moans, was all you could hear.

"Fuck..." he moaned as he exploded into me. "I bet not catch you out with another nigga again," he said as he laid next to me, and pulled me close.

"You won't," I smiled.

He climbed back on top of me, and kissed my lips.

My stomach had been killing me all night. I assumed it was because I was hungry, so I got up and ate some ice chips. That didn't work, but by 3 a.m. my body was dead tired and forced itself to sleep. I woke up early this morning, so that I could go and buy some breakfast. Afterwards, I planned to go hang out with Lucy, since Julius was being distant again.

"Good morning Dalia," I said as I walked into the living room.

"Morning," she replied, watching TV.

I walked over and sat down on the couch for a second. I wanted to watch a little free TV before getting my day started. I decided to send Julius a text for the 100th time this week, and see if I got a response. Ten minutes passed and as usual, I got nothing. I was getting tired of his antics. He talked to me only when he felt like it, and then if I talked to another guy he went ballistic. As much as I wanted to forget him, I couldn't. I wanted to cry every time I thought about him.

"What is that smell?" I turned my nose up as my mother walked to the kitchen.

"Sardines," she replied, throwing it away.

I immediately jumped up and ran to the bathroom. I flipped the toilet top open, and threw up violently. I hadn't ate much yesterday, so it soon just became stomach acid that I was throwing up. I sat there on the bathroom floor, panting and dry heaving. I looked up to see my mother standing in the doorway, with her arms folded.

"Natalia, you better not be pregnant," she glared down at me.

I shook my head no. "No, I haven't even been having sex," I lied.

"You think I don't know about you and Julius?" she raised a brow. I didn't respond for a couple seconds.

"He is just a friend. We haven't done anything," I said, assuring her and standing up.

"I hope so, because you know the deal. If you get pregnant, you get the fuck out," she said, and turned to leave the house. I nodded my head yes, although she had her back to me.

I closed the bathroom door and cried for a little bit. *I couldn't be pregnant, right?* I asked myself. This was the first time I threw up, so I didn't worry too much. I thought about every time I had sex with Julius; he never used a condom. I shook the negative thoughts from my head, brushed my teeth, and showered.

I needed to get a second opinion, because I felt my mom was just being paranoid. Once I finished showering, I went to Lucy's house so we could go eat breakfast at IHOP. I was so damn hungry, yet nervous about my current condition.

"Why are you so quiet, Natalia? Julius ain't dick you down last night?" Lucy chuckled as she stared at me.

I scrolled on my phone, hoping a call or text from Julius would come through, even though I knew he only called when he wanted some pussy. I shook my head, upset that I went from being a virgin to a booty call.

"Lucy, how did you know when you were pregnant?" I asked. Lucy had so many abortions that I footed the bill for that I'm sure she knew the signs.

"Why?" she frowned and cocked her head.

"Can you just tell me?" I asked with pleading eyes.

She paused for a moment. "Well, each time was different, because you react different with each dude's baby. Once, I was throwing up a lot; another time, I couldn't bear certain smells that usually didn't bother me; and another time, a smell made me throw up," she replied.

I blew out hot air, and folded my arms over my chest. "I think I'm pregnant, Lucy," I said, feeling tears well up.

"Oh my gosh. Did you take a test?" she asked.

"I ain't got enough for that bullshit," I replied, letting the tears fall. I quickly wiped them when the waiter brought our food over.

"You guys need anything else?" the waiter asked. We both shook our heads no, as I avoided eye contact with her.

"We can go to the clinic, and they will test you for free," Lucy smiled.

"Can you come with me?" I asked.

"I'm mad you even asked! You know I will." Lucy shook her head as she ate a slice of pancake.

I half smiled, and dug in as well.

"Natalia Thomas," the lady from the clinic smiled as she walked into the room.

"Yes, that's me," I smiled.

"Good, I have the right room," she smiled, and sat down. "So we tested you for STD's and HIV, which all came back negative," she smiled. "However, you are pregnant; 4 weeks," she said.

"I am. I see," I said, looking down.

"Yes, so what are your plans? Do you have any questions?" she smiled.

"How much is an abortion?" I asked, hoping it was cheaper than the ones I got Lucy.

"$200," she replied, killing my hopes.

"I-I am going to keep it," I stammered.

"Okay Ms. Thomas. I will write a prenatal vitamin prescription for you," she smiled.

"Thank you," I replied.

"What did she say?" Lucy asked as we walked to the bus stop.

"I'm 4 weeks," I replied.

"So what are you going to do?" she asked.

"I'm keeping it," I said somberly.

"What did Julius say?"

"I haven't told him. He hasn't talked to me in two weeks, so I'm gonna drop by," I said as we walked onto the bus. Lucy nodded, and rubbed my back.

I took the bus, and then walked a block to Julius' house. I hated that he had been ignoring me, but I needed him to know about the baby. As much as I wished I wasn't pregnant, I didn't want to kill my baby. I arrived to his house, and sat on his porch. I was going to wait until he came home, I didn't care how long it took. Two hours went by, and his black Lexus finally pulled up. He hopped out the car, and a girl got out the passenger seat. A huge lump formed in my throat, and my stomach began to hurt. I was angry, but more so hurt. He'd been ignoring me after spitting all that bullshit about wanting me, just to be with another bitch. He got closer and finally noticed me sitting there. I had my long, chestnut curly hair down, and was wearing jean shorts, my "keds," and a blue V-neck t-shirt.

"Who is this?" the girl asked.

"No who are you?!" I spat.

"Natalia, what you doing here ma?" Julius asked, walking up with the girl right behind him.

Tears spilled over my lower lids, as I could no longer hold them in. "What am I doing here? Why haven't you been answering my calls and texts?" I yelled through tears.

"Look man, I ain't got time for this shit. What you need to talk to me about?" he asked as he walked to his door and unlocked it. The girl and I followed him inside, and he told her to sit on the couch. He led me to his bedroom, and then closed the door. "Speak," he said.

"I'm pregnant," I said.

"By who?" he asked.

I was so shocked I could barely speak. "You know I have only been with you." I felt myself crying hard again.

"How I know? I ain't seen you in weeks," he shrugged.

"Because you don't answer your phone! I hate you! You used me knowing you never cared about me!" I cried, hating him for being an asshole, and myself for being so damn dumb.

He didn't say anything, and reached in his pocket. He pulled out a wad of money, and peeled off a couple hundreds. "How much to get rid of it, if it is mine?" he raised a brow.

My legs all of a sudden felt like spaghetti, and a sharp pain shot through my chest. I loved this man so much, and he was treating me like some slut he picked up off the street. All the things he told me just to get between my legs were lies.

"$150 enough?" he added since I hadn't responded.

"$350," I lied. Since he played me, I was gonna play him.

"Aight here is $400," he said, and handed it to me. I was so shocked by his actions, but even more shocked that I still loved him. I wanted him to say he loved me and didn't mean the things he was saying, but I knew he wouldn't.

I took the money, and turned around to leave the bedroom. He came behind me, and hugged me tight. He kissed the back of my head, and inhaled the scent of my hair. He leaned down and kissed my cheek, then my neck and shoulder.

"I wish you knew what I was going through," he whispered.

"Get off me," I said calmly, as tears raced down my cheeks.

He tightened his grip around me, and rubbed my flat stomach under my shirt. His touch felt so good, and all the things he had just said to me didn't matter. He kissed my neck and I leaned my head back, basking in the moment.

"Julius!" the bitch he brought over yelled.

I nudged him off me and left.

I didn't want to treat Natalia that way, but I couldn't be with her. She was a little girl, and I was a 19-year-old man. I needed to be with bitches my age. I know y'all saying I should've thought about that before I fucked her but shit, she was so beautiful and her personality was refreshing. I was used to being around these artificial ass bitches, who were only worth the labels they sported. Natalia was different, and it made me like her little ass. I avoided her as much as I could, but at times I would have relapses. I licked my lips as I thought about her cute, petite, 5'5 frame, long light brown hair, her sexy honey complexion, and full lips. I stopped immediately, because all in all she and I could never be. If that baby was mine, I needed her to get it scraped out immediately. I was too damn busy to have a baby by someone I didn't want to be with; well, couldn't be with.

"You good?" this chick named Daphne asked. She was Bianca's "best friend," but as you can see, she wasn't much of a friend. She rubbed my bare back as she lay there, ass naked in my bed.

"Yeah I'm straight," I said, looking over my shoulder.

"You ready for another round?" she asked as she massaged my shoulders. I felt her titties lightly sweeping across my back.

"Nah, but you can give me some head," I replied.

She happily jumped to the floor, and took me into her mouth. She bobbed up and down, taking my full 11-inches with no problem. She had no gag reflexes, and it was the main reason I even started fucking with her. I knew it was shady as hell to fuck Bianca's best friend but shit, in my eyes, I belonged to no bitch. These hoes were shady as hell out here, that's why I wasn't about to let Natalia put her baby on me. Yeah, I hit raw on multiple occasions, but I knew how these chicks worked. Soon as you popped they cherry for them, they was out letting every nigga hit. They came to you to open the can of soda, and then let everyone else sip out of it. *That nigga I caught her in the car with had his tongue all down her throat, so I know he smashed,* I scoffed out loud at my thoughts. My blood boiled at the thought of whoever he was sticking his dick in Natalia.

"Fuck," I moaned as I felt myself about to bust down Daphne's throat. Daphne smiled with my dick still planted deep in her larynx damn near, as I threw my head back. "Shit," I said as I felt myself bust in her mouth.

"Mmmm that tasted good daddy," Daphne smiled and licked her lips.

I hopped up to take a shower, hoping to clear Natalia and that baby out of my mind.

***

"Aye, is that Ma?" my brother Rashad asked me.

I looked over as I continued to drive, and shook my head. "Yeah, that's her ass," I replied.

My mother had been on drugs since forever. My brother and I had acted like we didn't know her for years. It still made me feel some type of way seeing her, but I had to brush it off.

"I hate seeing her like this, man," Rashad commented. I didn't say anything, cause I refused to feel bad for her trifling ass.

"So what's up with the operation you setting up?" my boy Menzo asked from the backseat.

"Everything is going as planned, and don't worry, I'm putting y'all on," I smiled as I thought about my plans. I had one more meeting with a connect, and then everything would be set. Most of the time I was MIA., I was setting up in my soon to be new location, in South Carolina.

"How does Hugo feel?" my brother Rashad asked.

"It don't matter how he feel. He just needs to be happy I ain't setting up out here in Indiana," I frowned, and Rashad laughed.

"So you ain't gon' tell him?" Menzo asked.

"Yeah I am–when I get ready. If he wants a war after that, then so be it," I shrugged, not giving a fuck.

I wasn't scared of nobody on this damn Earth. Only thing I feared was God, and it had been that way since I was little. If you put your pants on one leg at a time like me, I wasn't scared of you. That's what made Hugo put me on in the first place; he knew I wasn't to be fucked with.

My phone had been ringing constantly between Bianca, Daphne, Natalia, and some bitch I just dicked down named Madelyn. I shook my head and exhaled heavily once I heard it go off. I ain't gon' lie, I smiled a little when I looked down and saw Natalia's name.

"What up?" I asked as I pulled over into the parking lot of the Castleton Square Mall.

"I don't think I can do it," Natalia sobbed on the other end. I waited until Rashad and Menzo exited the car before responding.

"You ain't got a choice, Nat. If that baby is mine and you have it, I'm putting you in the ground," I spat.

"I wish it wasn't yours! I hate you," she cried.

"Shit, it probably ain't. Now get it done," I said, and disconnected. If Natalia was pregnant by me and had it, I wouldn't dare hurt her, but I needed her to think that so that she *would* get rid of it.

"You good?" Rashad asked as I exited the car.

"Spiffy," I chuckled, and so did he.

"Girl, I drove by and she was waiting on his porch," Daphne said as she took a pull on the blunt.

"I warned that bitch," I said

Julius had been ignoring me ever since I walked in on him and Natalia. I felt slightly bad for her, cause her nose was busted and I knew Julius had been hitting her. What was most surprising was that this nigga had just got done eating her pussy. For the two years we had been together, this nigga swore up and down he didn't eat pussy. I knew he did it to her, because I heard her moaning and when I walked in, he was kissing up her stomach.

"So what you gon' do?" Daphne asked me, snapping me out of my trip down memory lane.

"I got something for that bitch. I know just how to get back at her and get my man talking to me again," I chuckled.

"Why you even want him still?" Daphne frowned.

"Cause I love his crazy ass," I admitted.

"After all he's done to you? Where is your pride?" she scoffed.

"Pride and love don't mix, Daphne," I simply replied. She rolled her eyes and shook her head.

Daphne hated Julius for how he treated me. Every time he did something to me, she wanted me to leave him. I appreciated her being a great friend and caring, but she needed to just stay out of it. I loved Julius, and I knew we could work through this bullshit. I just needed to get Natalia's annoying ass out the way.

I watched as that stupid home-wrecking bitch walked out of her school. Although a stripper, I was a great ass actress. Soon as she started walking by my car, I rolled down my window to get her attention. She looked sad as hell, as she held onto the straps of her backpack. I was happy her little friend Lucy wasn't with her, cause that would ruin my plan.

"Natalia!" I called out.

"Bianca?" she turned to look at me.

"Come here for a second," I smiled. She hesitated and looked around. "Natalia, I'm not gonna do anything. I just want to talk, woman to woman," I smiled.

She hesitated, and then got into my car. I cranked it up, and pulled away from the curb. "Wait where are we going?" she asked.

"Just for a drive. I hate sitting in cars, people get shot like that," I replied and she didn't say anything. "I wanted to make amends with you, Natalia." I started.

"You do? Why?" she asked.

"Cause I realized it wasn't your fault that Julius and I's relationship fell apart. I should've been let him go," I lied. It definitely was this bitch's fault. Yeah, Julius fucked around all the time, but he never went as far as he has with Natalia.

"Oh. I'm sorry Bianca, he told me you guys were broken up. I didn't try to fall in love with him," she whined. *Yeah right bitch.*

"I know boo. It's cool though, I'm over Julius and the situation," I waved my hand in the air. "So, what do you say to a truce?" I asked.

"That sounds good," she smiled.

"We haven't hung out in awhile, why don't we chill and talk some more," I said.

"Okay," she smiled. She was so dumb; I actually almost felt bad for her.

We got to my apartment, and headed upstairs to my door. When we walked in, Greg and his friend Ynez were chilling on the couch just as planned.

"Natalia!" Greg smiled.

"Hey," she replied dryly. They couldn't stand each other.

"This my boy Ynez," Greg said, and Natalia waved and half smiled.

"Want a drink?" I asked her once she sat down.

"No. I-I ca- don't want anything," she stuttered. I shrugged my shoulders, and made Greg, Ynez, and I a drink.

After a while of drinking and good conversation, I gave Greg a look, letting him know it was time to take my plan into action. *Greg would do anything for some cash*, I thought. He nodded and sipped his drink.

"Damn, Bianca can you take me to the bank? I need to get some cash for my moms," Greg said.

"Aight come on," I said, standing up and fixing my jeans. I noticed Natalia stood up too, attempting to leave with us. "Oh we will be right back Natalia," I told her.

"I think I should get home anyway, I have homework," she half smiled.

"Don't be a party pooper. We haven't hung out in forever. Stay put until we get back from the bank," I smiled. She hesitated, and then sat back down. I winked at Ynez, and then left with Greg.

I wish Bianca hadn't left me here alone with Ynez, but I didn't want to upset her and make her think I wasn't trying to be friends. I mean, why not be cool with her? It was clear Julius didn't care about me like I thought he did.

"So Natalia, how old are you?" Ynez asked, smirking at me.

"I'm 16, until April 28th," I replied fidgeting.

"Damn, only 16. You're beautiful," he commented.

"Thank you," I half smiled.

Ynez got up and sat next to me. He leaned back and threw his arm along the back of the couch. He smelled like strong weed and gin.

"Damn, even better up close," he said, licking his lips. I didn't respond, because I felt uncomfortable.

"I'm gonna catch the bus home," I said, standing up.

"Chill ma, I ain't gon' bite," he said.

I stared down at him, and then sat back down. Once I did, he scooted closer to me, invading my personal space. He started kissing my neck, and I tried pushing him off but he was too strong. He grabbed my wrists and threw them back, making me fall back onto the couch. He got between my legs, and started kissing my neck.

"Please stop!" I yelled and squirmed.

"Calm yo ass down, and stop acting like you don't give the pussy up!" Ynez spat. He held my wrists so tight that I'm sure my blood stopped circulating.

"Please stop! I'm pregnant!" I told him.

He paused, and stared into my face. He hopped up off me, and I sat up touching my wrists. I hopped up to leave, and met Bianca and Greg standing outside the door.

"You ain't tell me this bitch was pregnant!" Ynez spat.

"This hoe ain't pregnant!" Bianca yelled.

"Yes I am!" I yelled, looking into her mischievous eyes. She planned all this shit.

I stormed out the apartment, and Greg grabbed my ass as I did. I turned around and slapped his ass in the face, hard as hell. He just grabbed his cheek and laughed.

"This ain't over Natalia!" Bianca yelled after me.

I ran to the bus stop, as tears fell down my face. I couldn't believe Bianca tried to set me up. What if I wasn't pregnant? That nigga would've raped me right there. I finally got on the bus to head home, and I dialed Julius. He didn't answer as usual, and I started to cry even more.

Me: *Head to my house. I need to talk.*

Lucy Bff: *Okay.*

I finally got home, and I saw Lucy sitting on the stone wall outside my apartment complex. I grabbed her hand, and ran up to my door.

"Dalia?" I called out to see if my mother was home. I got no answer, and plopped down on the couch.

"Okay, what's up Nat?" Lucy asked, sitting down as well.

"Bianca tried to get me raped," I said.

"What? How? Why?" she asked, looking confused.

"She tried to make me believe we were cool, and then left me at her apartment with some guy. He almost raped me until I told him about the baby," I said, looking down.

"We need to fuck her up," Lucy frowned.

"After the abortion," I replied exhaling.

"So you're gonna get it?" she asked, and I nodded my head. "Damn. When?"

"This Saturday," I replied.

JULIUS

"So that bitch is pregnant?!" Bianca screamed at me, as I sat on my bed.

"Nah," I replied, not giving a fuck.

Bianca and I's relationship had been soured, and I wasn't sure why I hadn't just broke up with her ass already. Only reason we was together now was because I wanted some pussy, but I was about to say fuck it and leave.

"I heard she was, Julius!" she yelled.

"Man, lower your fucking voice! If she is pregnant, what the fuck you gon' do about it?" I frowned.

"I don't want you fucking with her! Not like this! You doing too much!" she yelled through tears.

"Ain't nobody fucking with her! If she pregnant, it prolly ain't mine," I shrugged as I slid on my tennis shoes.

"Where you going?" she asked.

"I came for some pussy and head, not all this mouth," I said, tying my shoe.

"Wait, aight. I'm sorry Julius. When I heard she was pregnant, I panicked," she said in a calmer tone.

She walked over to me and dropped to her knees to suck my dick. Once I nutted down her throat, she climbed on the bed and spread her legs.

"Is today my lucky day?" she smiled.

"I don't do that, and if you keep asking me, I'm not gon' fuck with you no more," I spat.

When was she gon' get the hint? I wasn't munching on her shit, or anyone else's. I surprised myself when I did it to Natalia. Her pussy was so pretty, and I just wanted to taste her–don't ask me why. As they say, it's always that one person that will make you try anything.

"You ate that bitch out!" Bianca frowned.

"Aight, peace," I replied, putting my dick back up.

"Wait! Julius!" she yelled after me, but I ignored her stupid ass.

My phone buzzed, and I saw I had a text from Daphne. I hoped she was available, because I needed some pussy and Bianca was tripping. I was refraining from contacting Natalia, because fucking her was starting to become too emotional for me. I felt like I was making love and I ain't like that; plus, I didn't want her to think me smashing meant keep the baby.

Daphne: *Wyd?*

Me: *In need of some pussy.*

I wanted to get straight to the point.

Daphne: *Come thru.*

Me: *Fasho.*

I decided to hit up Natalia, to check the status on that damn abortion. I needed her to take care of that, and not play games.

Me: *Have you took care of your problem?*

Natalia: *My problem?*

Me: *Did you take care of it or not?*

Natalia: *I go tomorrow. Can you pick me up? They said I shouldn't walk home.*

Me: *You can ride the bus. Let me know when it's done.*

Natalia: *I hate you.*

Me: *I'll be waiting on confirmation from ya.*

I shook my head at her emotional ass. If that baby wasn't out of her stomach by tomorrow evening, I was gon' have to find a way to get it out myself. These hoes kill me man. I sped off and headed to Daphne's to bang her out.

I cried all night, as I re-read Julius and I's conversation. Why was he treating me this way? Whatever; no matter how much I loved him, I needed to get over it.

I got up, showered, and brushed my teeth. I decided to wear a simple black dress that was t-shirt material. I put my long brown hair into a bun on top of my head, and headed out to catch the bus.

"Are you ready Natalia?" the doctor asked, and I nodded.

O nce the procedure was done, I went ahead and started to get dressed. I was so sore, and knew walking home was gonna be a challenge. The bus could only get me so close to home, so I would still have to walk a ways.

Me: It's done Julius, can you please pick me up. I'm in pain.

I waited about ten minutes, and got no response. I took a deep breath to hold the tears in. I saw a nurse approaching me, as I stood up.

"Do you have a ride home, Natalia?" she asked.

"Yes, they're outside," I lied.

I rode the bus as close to my house as it could get, then got off to walk the rest of the way. I wanted to cry, because I was in so much pain. A lot of time had passed, and Julius still hadn't texted me back. I hated him, and still loved him at the same time. Tears finally escaped my eyes, due to the pain I was experiencing. I was walking extremely slow, and home seemed so far away.

"Well look who it is," Bianca walked up on me, with two other girls.

"I'm not in the mood Bianca. You can have Julius," I replied calmly, trying to walk around her. Her friend stopped me in my tracks.

"I don't need you to tell me that! And bitch don't act like you giving him to me!" Bianca yelled, and pushed me back.

"Ahh," I groaned in pain. "Please Bianca, I can't do this right now. Julius and I haven't been together in almost a month," I whined.

"Too late to plead your case," she said as she punched me.

Because of the pain I was in, my legs weakened under me and I fell. The other two girls began kicking and stomping on me all over, as Bianca rained blows down on my face. I had no energy or strength to stop them, and laid there helplessly crying.

"Back the fuck up!" I heard Julius yell.

The constant punches and kicks ceased, and I laid there feeling paralyzed.

"Julius. Hey babe," Bianca said.

"Fuck outta here," Julius spat, as he picked me up bridal style.

"Leave that hoe here, Julius!" Bianca yelled, following behind him.

"Get the fuck back for I fuck you up," Julius said through gritted teeth.

"That's who you want, Julius! This young bitch! Fuck you, you cradle robber!" Bianca yelled, as Julius placed me in his passenger seat.

He closed the door, and turned around to slap the shit out of her. She grabbed her face, and stared up at him with a hate-filled expression. I wanted to get out of his car, but the pain from the procedure and that ass kicking was too much.

"You and I are a fucking wrap!" Julius yelled, as he jogged to the driver side.

"Julius wait!" she yelled as he sped off.

The car ride was silent as I stared out the window. My life was bad enough before Julius, and he just seemed to make it worse.

"How you feeling, Nat?" he finally broke the silence. I said nothing as I continued to stare out the window. "Natalia. Baby I'm sorry I didn't pick you up," he added.

"Just take me home please," I replied as my face became drenched with tears.

He didn't reply, and continued to drive to my apartment complex. Once we arrived, he pulled over and shut off the engine. I sat up slowly, and winced in pain.

"Let me help you," he said as he hopped out and jogged to my side.

He picked me up out the car, and carried me up to my apartment. He let me down, and I slowly took my key out to open the door. I walked slow as hell to the bathroom, and attempted to run me a bath.

"Ahh," I cried as my body ached. I wanted to beat Bianca's ass, but knew I was in no condition obviously.

"I got it ma," Julius said as he stepped in the bathroom to turn the water knobs.

Once it started to fill up, he helped me undress slowly and once I was naked, he started to place kisses on my flat stomach. I pushed him away lightly, with what little strength I had. He then picked me up, and put me in the tub gently.

"Thanks. You can leave," I commented as I laid back in the tub.

"You want me to leave?" he asked, like an idiot. I nodded my head with my eyes closed. "Natalia, I said I was sorry I-"

"You treated me like shit! Stop acting like you care now! Please get out and never talk to me again, please," I cried.

"Natalia you-"

"I don't understand. I know. Goodbye, Julius," I said, turning my head.

He started to say something, but decided against it. Once I heard the front door slam, I broke down into tears. Never talking to Julius again was gonna make my life much better.

TWO MONTHS LATER

Natalia meant what she said, and stuck by it. I had text and called her constantly, and she never responded. I tried to give her a ride to school, but she walked right by me as if she didn't know me.

It was her 17th birthday, and I wanted to do something nice for her. I didn't know why I wanted her back in my life, when I knew I wasn't gonna be with her. Yeah I wanted her, but she was turning 17 and I was gonna be 20 June 8th; that wouldn't look right, but damn did I miss her pretty ass.

Bianca had been blowing me up, and I was ignoring her as usual. I was still smashing Daphne, and this new chick named Franceska. You'd think I was good but no, Natalia consumed my thoughts.

"Natalia!" I called out as she walked out of school. She kept walking and looking straight ahead. She looked so good in light blue skinny jeans that accentuated her little plump ass, a white tube top showing her toned stomach, and white sandals. Her long light brown hair was pressed, with a part on the side.

I hopped out my car and grabbed her arm, which she snatched. "Baby, let me just take you out to dinner," I said.

"Why? So you can take me home, fuck me, and then ignore me for some weeks?" she asked. Her facial expression was filled with hurt.

"No, just dinner. I will take you to eat, and then home if that's what you want," I replied.

"For what?" she frowned.

"It's your birthday," I smiled.

"You remembered my birthday?" she asked, and I nodded. She paused as if she was thinking about it. "No, Julius. All you want to do is get me in your bed. You don't care about me," she said as a single tear ran down her face.

"Natal-"

"No!" she yelled

"You been fucking with another nigga?" I frowned.

"Maybe," She spat. I slapped the shit out of her, and her lip busted immediately.

"Natalia babe I'm-"

"Just, leave me alone Julius," she said calmly, and rushed off.

"Fuck!" I yelled once I got in the car.

I was done trying to make amends with her ass. Fuck Natalia.

I heard a lot of commotion and sirens outside my complex, so I threw on a dress and ran downstairs. There was an ambulance truck, and of course everyone was standing around being nosey.

"What happened?" I asked my neighbor Diane.

"Just another damn overdose," she scoffed.

"Did you know them?" I asked.

"Yeah, we used to be cool a looong time ago, but she started smoking dope," she said, shaking her head as the EMT's rolled the black body bag to their truck. "Tina really lost her mind," she added, and turned to leave.

"Tina Tate?" I asked and she nodded, then walked back into our complex.

I remembered Julius telling me his mother's name was Tina, so I ran back upstairs to get my phone and house keys. As much as I hated his guts, I wanted to make sure he was okay. Just cause he didn't give a fuck about me, didn't mean I should treat him the same. As a wise person once said, two wrongs don't make a right.

I got off the bus, and headed down the block to Julius' house. *I probably should've text him, and made sure he was home,* I thought. I let out a sigh of relief as I reached his house and spotted his car. I walked up the walkway, and saw his door was open behind the screen. I pulled the screen open, and then closed the door behind me.

"Julius?" I called out and heard nothing.

I continued walking through the house, until I reached his room. It was slightly cracked, and I heard light sniffles. I slowly opened the door, making him jump. He wiped his face quickly with his shirt, as he sat on the bed.

"Natalia, what's up? What you doing here?" he asked and sniffled once more.

"I came to check on you," I said walking in, and slowly closing the bedroom door behind me.

"Oh, I'm good. How are you?" he forced a smile.

"No, I came to check on you because I heard about your mother," I replied.

"Oh, I'm straight. We haven't been close since I was 13," he chuckled lightly.

I stared into his eyes, seeing how sad he was. He didn't say anything as we stared at one another for a couple seconds. I walked closer to him, and pulled him into a hug. He wrapped his arms around my waist, burying his head in my stomach. He broke down crying and I just held him, letting him get it all out.

"I loved my mama, Nat. She did my brother and I dirty, but I loved her. She was a good mom for 13 years of my life," he cried harder with every word.

After crying for a couple minutes, he stopped and wiped his face. I sat next to him on the bed, and turned his face to me. Before I could speak, he leaned me back on the bed and dipped his tongue in my mouth. He rubbed his hand up my dress, tugging on my panties.

"Julius wai-"

"I care about you Natalia. I wanna be with you, ma. I realized life is too short," he said, as if he read my mind.

He dipped his tongue in my mouth, and continued to pull my panties down. He climbed on top of me, between my legs, and pulled my dress over my head. He removed his shirt, and I admired his abs, chest, and strong arms. His peanut butter complexion was flawless as usual. He stepped out of his jeans and boxers, then climbed back on the bed. After planting kisses from my lips to my naval, he took my clit into his mouth. He lifted my legs on his shoulders, without breaking his rhythm.

"Julius…" I moaned as I palmed the back of his head. He pushed my legs back, and sucked harder until I came. He lapped it up like a thirsty dog. He kissed back up my body, and then positioned the head of his dick at my opening. "You have a condom?" I asked.

"I need to feel you, Nat," he replied, and dipped his tongue in my mouth.

He slowly entered me and lifted my legs over his biceps, as he thrusted into me in a circular motion. It was slightly painful, since we hadn't had sex in almost four months.

"I love you, Natalia," he said.

"You do?" I asked. He nodded and tongued me down. "I love you too, Julius," I moaned.

He sped up, making me cum hard as hell. He let my legs down, and wrapped his arms around my petite frame, holding me close. We kissed non-stop as he continued to stroke me.

"You my girl officially, aight? My only girl," he said, and it was music to my ears.

"No Bianca?" I moaned.

"Nah, just Natalia and Julius," he replied as he continued to hit my spot.

I hate to admit it, but a nigga was feeling good as hell having Natalia on my arm. I really tried, I really did, to keep her away. My mom dying made me realize that life is too short to not be with the person you want. Also, the fact that she made it all the way to my crib to check on me when my mother died made me want her even more. Bianca text me about it, as well as Daphne, but neither one of them came to my aide; and them hoes had cars. Not like I wanted them to, but damn.

"I want to take you shopping at the mall, since you said you've never been able to," I said to Natalia as she put her long brown hair in a ponytail. She had on dark blue jean shorts, a yellow tube top showing her sexy flat stomach, and brown sandals. Although she clearly didn't wear labels, she still looked better than the bitches that did. "Where you want to go?" I asked, walking up behind her and hugging her small frame.

"To Kroger," she replied.

"The grocery store?" I frowned, and turned her to face me.

"Yes, please. I won't get a lot," she replied.

"Why you wanna go there, ma?" I was confused as hell.

"Eating fast food is breaking my pockets, so I'd rather have food at home that I can cook. That way I can have leftovers and stuff," she replied.

"Natalia, you don't have food at home?" I asked, and she shook her head.

"What the hell does your sister eat?" I frowned.

"She has a better job, and she always eats out with her friends or boyfriend at the time," she said.

I was silent for a moment in disbelief. No wonder she had to steal and shit. No wonder she wouldn't let me waste food at restaurants.

"Aight, we can go to Kroger babe. And I want you to get as much stuff as you want, don't worry about the cost, aight?" I said.

"Okay, thank you Julius!" she smiled as if I said she won the lottery, and it broke my heart.

Knowing that she lived at home where she had no food angered me. I'd much rather her live here, where I knew she wouldn't go hungry, but I didn't know if I was ready for all that. I was just gonna take her grocery shopping every other weekend, to make sure she was good though.

Before the grocery store, she wanted to go to Target. She wanted to get some new bedding and other accessories for her bedroom, because what she had was in bad shape. Finding this out made me wonder what kind of sister would live like a Queen, knowing her sibling was living like a peasant and starving. Natalia refused to let me buy her clothes and things, because she said she didn't need it. I was still going to buy her some sort of late birthday gift regardless. I didn't like that she walked and caught the bus everywhere, so maybe I'd get her a car.

We dropped the groceries and Target shit off, and decided to go dinner. We agreed on Bazbeaux's, because we both had a taste for pizza.

"Thank you for all the stuff. I will pay it-"

"No you won't. I don't want your money," I replied.

"I can pay for my own stuff, once I save," she smiled. I admired her beauty a bit before responding.

"I know you can, ma. I would be insulted if you paid me back though," I smiled, and so did she.

"Did you really mean it when you said you loved me?" she asked.

"Yeah I did. Why?" I raised a brow.

"Cause you would never say it back when I used to say it, so I was just wondering," she replied shrugging.

I grabbed her hand, and kissed the back of it. "Nah, I didn't want to be in love to be honest. But I love you Natalia, and I wouldn't say it if I didn't mean it."

"Oh I know," she raised both brows, and we laughed.

"Julius, hi," Daphne said, walking up. She had on a tight ass dress, Louboutin boots, and a Louis Vuitton bag hanging from her forearm.

"What's up Daph?" I replied, and cleared my throat.

"I see you're doing all you can to help the community," she smiled.

"What?" I frowned in confusion.

"Well you're sitting here with a troubled youth. Giving back, I like it," Daphne chuckled, as she looked at Natalia.

"I'm not a troubled youth, I'm his girlfriend," Natalia said with confidence.

"Ha! His girlfriend? Is that what he told you so he can fuck?" Daphne chuckled.

"No, that's what I told her cause it's true. Now get yo ass away from over here with yo jealous ass," I shook my head, irritated as hell.

"Damn, like that Julius?" Daphne frowned.

"Just like that. And don't ever disrespect my girl like that again," I replied, staring into her envious eyes. She paused with her mouth ajar, and then stormed away. "Don't mind her baby," I said to Natalia.

"I'm fine," she smiled.

"You sure?" I asked. I expected her to be mad at me.

"Yeah, I'm glad you told her what it was," she replied. I smiled at her answer.

Every minute I spent with her seemed to confirm more and more that she was wifey. She was young, but seemed to be more level headed, humble, and logical than the older hoes I dated.

Daphne: *Damn, why you diss me like that?*

Me: *Fuck off.*

Daphne: *Julius, I'm sorry baby.*

I didn't reply, and locked my phone. Our food arrived, and we started to dig in. The shit was bomb as usual, and I was stuffed. Once we left, we headed to her apartment, where I helped set up the new stuff for her room.

"Let's christen these sheets," I smiled.

I picked her up, and she wrapped her legs around my waist. We pressed our lips against one another's, and then I dipped my tongue in her mouth. I laid her on the bed, and she kicked off her sandals. I tugged down her jean shorts and panties together, then placed her toned caramel thighs on my shoulders.

"You so fucking sexy Nat," I moaned as I planted kisses from her naval to her lower lips.

I licked between the slit, and she arched her back. This girl had me eating her pussy like it was the cure to a cancer I had. Bitches didn't get this treatment, but for some reason I loved the taste of Natalia.

"Uhhhh, Juli- ahhhh," she moaned as she rubbed her soft hands over my curls. I loved when she did that.

I spread her legs some more, and then lifted them off my shoulders a bit for more access. I sucked her clit harder, and slowly dipped my tongue in her hole. I did that back and forth, until she came twice. I could eat her all damn day, which is a lot to say for Julius Tate.

"Baby, I-I can't take anymorrrree, ahhhh," she moaned as she came again.

She tried to scoot away, so I locked down her bottom half. She propped herself up on her elbows, and threw her head back in ecstasy. Her body shook violently, and she released again. I sucked up every drop, and then kissed my way up to her soft lips. She shivered under my body, and then lightly pushed me on my back.

"Natalia, you don't have to- Fuck," I moaned as she took me into her mouth. "Sloppy just like that ma, damn," I moaned as she played with my balls and sucked me off.

I wondered where she learned this shit, cause I knew she had never done it. She sped up her pace, and I lightly grabbed her long hair. Soon enough, I busted all down her throat. I immediately hopped up, and put her on her back. I placed her legs over my shoulders, and entered her slowly.

"Ooohhh," we both moaned in unison. I pumped nice and slow in a circular motion, as we kissed hard.

"I'm about to cum already Nat, damn," I said.

"I'm cumming baby!" she moaned, and released over my shaft.

Her pussy was now wetter, and I couldn't take it any longer. I eased in her fast, and pulled out slowly. Finally, my stomach muscles tightened, and I released into her. I dropped down closer to her, and we tongued each other down. Natalia could get me to do anything she wanted with this pussy. *Damn.*

I got home around 1 a.m., because Natalia's sister text and said she was on her way. She acted like her sister was her mom almost; maybe she was just over protective. That was another reason I wanted her move in. I needed to be able to be with her for as long as I wanted. *Maybe I will buy her a nice apartment,* I thought as I hit the alarm on my car.

"Julius!"

I turned around to see Bianca, and blew out hot air. She wore tights, and a t-shirt, and her hair was down. Her red weave looked slightly disheveled, but she was still pretty nonetheless.

"What's up?" I replied, folding my arms and checking behind her.

"I wanted to talk," she replied.

"About what?" I asked.

"Us."

"There ain't no *us*, Bianca. Hasn't been for almost three months now when you decided to jump Natalia, and get crazy out your mouth with me," I scoffed.

"I know, that was dumb to jump her. I was just in my feelings," she replied.

"Whatever. Goodnight Bianca," I said, turning around to walk to my door.

"Is it true you're with Natalia now?" she asked, following me.

"Why? What does it matter?" I frowned, walking into my crib. Unfortunately, she followed.

"Because you promised me nothing serious was going on between you two," she said, folding her arms.

I shook my head, and shut my front door. She sat on my couch, and I went to my fridge to retrieve the Jack Daniels my older brother copped for me. I grabbed a glass, added some ice, and headed back to my living room.

"So is it true?" she said.

"Yep," I replied, pouring some liquor into my glass. I sat the bottle on the glass coffee table, and then took a sip from my glass.

Bianca shook her head, then stood up off the couch. She walked over to me, and dropped to her knees. She slid her small hands up my jeans, and unzipped them.

"Does she suck your dick like this?" she asked as she started to suck on the head like a vacuum.

"Damn," I moaned, and sipped my drink again.

Bianca bobbed up and down, taking all 11 inches into her mouth. I felt her tonsils, and that shit turned me on.

"Mmmm," she moaned as if it tasted good.

I grabbed the back of her head, and slowly humped upward in her face. She took every stroke like a pro. I felt my nut rising, and I let loose in her mouth. She swallowed every drop, and stood up to remove her shirt. I grabbed her roughly, and bent her over the couch arm. I tugged her tights down to her knees, and then pulled a condom out my wallet. I grabbed a fistful of her hair, and then plowed into her hard and fast. The smacking of our skin and her loud moans could be heard miles away. I sped up, cause I wanted to get my nut and send her home.

"Fuck Julius! Aahhhh, I'm cumming," she moaned, and scrunched up her face. "I love you so much," she added.

She came and collapsed on the couch arm. I smacked her ass hard, and then pulled out. I removed the condom, and nutted on her ass cheeks. I hopped up, and went to get her a warm, soapy paper towel so she could clean herself. Usually I would clean her off, but she wasn't my bitch no more.

"Here," I said, and she paused.

"Damn, I gotta do it myself now?" she frowned.

I didn't answer, and picked up my iPhone to look at it. I lit a blunt, then plopped down on the couch to check the notifications. I had a couple texts from my boy Menzo, my brother Rashad, Daphne's annoying ass, and my baby Natalia.

Baby Girl Nat: *Goodnight babe. I love you.*

Me: *Goodnight baby, I love you too.*

Baby Girl Nat: *Don't forget the movies tomorrow.*

Me: *I won't.*

"Damn, she got you smiling like that?" Bianca spat. I didn't even realize I was cheesing hard until she said something.

"Man, go home," I turned my lip up, and then took a pull on my blunt.

"You love her, Julius?" Bianca asked with a shaken voice. I looked away from my phone to her, and saw a tear running down her light cheeks.

"That's what the fuck you get for being nosey. Saw some shit you didn't wanna see," I spat. I stood up, and opened the front door for her. "You gotta go, I'm about to shower," I said.

She scoffed, and shook her head. She stood up and walked past me out the door. She turned around to face me, and her cheeks were drenched in tears.

"I was with you for two years, and you've never told me you loved me," she stated.

"We wasn't meant, ma. Have a goodnight," I shrugged.

She stared at me for a bit, then headed to her car. I slammed the door, and then headed to shower.

NATALIA

1 MONTH LATER

R*ed or Pink?* I asked myself. I started to paint my nails, and I heard the front door slam. I listened as the fridge doors were opened, and then closed. I bobbed my head to the Amina Buddafly CD I was listening to, as I finished painting my nails in red. My phone played Lady In a Glass Dress, letting me know I had a text. I smiled when I realized it was Julius.

Boyfriend: *I miss you beautiful.*

Me: *You just saw me yesterday.*

I smiled at my phone.

Boyfriend: *Be at my house by 7 ma. Pack an overnight bag.*

Me: *Okay.*

"Where did all that damn food come from?" my mother Dalia busted into my room.

"The fridge has been fully stocked like that for a month now," I replied. Julius had been taking me grocery shopping every other weekend to make sure I had food. I wasn't sure why she was just now asking.

"I know that. I'm asking you where the hell it came from," she glared at me as she leaned on my door.

"My check," I lied.

"Natalia, your check is about $100 plus bucks. The amount of food in there is about $300 worth. Where the fuck did it come from? And whose car is that in my extra parking spot in the garage? Where did that come from?!" she frowned, and folded her arms over her chest.

"J-Julius," I stuttered, as I twisted the cap back on the nail polish.

"You fucking him?" she asked, and I quickly shook my head no. "You telling me that he's filling our fridge with food, and bought you a brand new Honda Accord, just because he likes you? Get the fuck out of here, Natalia! I know the game boo, and the only reason a man buys a car is because he's getting some pussy!" she yelled, angry as hell.

"I'm not sleeping with him," I lied again.

She stormed into my room, and reached for my phone. "Brand new iPhone, Natalia?" she raised a brow, and I didn't say anything. She grabbed a box of tampons, and threw them at me. "I know you fucking now! You claimed you couldn't use these for years, and now you can?" she glared at me. "Well let me tell you this, if you come home pregnant, you better hope that nigga moves you in you little slut, because you getting the fuck out of here!" she yelled, and slapped the shit out of me.

"I won't, I'm not having sex!" I lied again.

She turned to leave, and then turned back around and punched me. I flew back on the bed, and grabbed my face. A little bit of blood started to drip from my nose as she walked out of my room. I ran to the bathroom and cleaned my nose up. I went to my room, packed a bag, slid on my shoes, and headed out. I hopped in my car, sped to Julius' house, and prayed that he was there. Once I arrived, I hopped out the car and ran to beat on his door.

"Natalia, what happened ma?" Julius answered the door, and I rushed into him. He hugged me tight, and then pulled back a bit. "What happened to your face?" he frowned.

"My mother hit me," I cried.

"Your mother? I thought you said you didn't know your mother?" he asked confused.

"My sister isn't my sister, she *is* my mom," I cried.

He kissed my lips a couple times, then closed and locked his front door. He picked me up bridal style, and then took me to his room. He laid me down, and then climbed in bed next to me. He had on a white t-shirt, black basketball shorts, and socks on. His short curly hair was freshly cut, and his cologne was still prevalent. I was so in love with him.

"What happened?" he asked, and kissed my cheek.

"She saw the food, the car, and the phone. She hit me cause she found out we had sex," I replied embarrassed. I knew he had a problem with my age, and here I was getting a *"spankin"* for having sex.

"She just hatin," he smiled, and kissed my lips.

"Yeah," I replied and smiled. We intertwined our fingers, and stared at our hands in the air. "Even our hands look perfect together," I chuckled, and so did he.

"I'm hungry, wanna go out?" he asked.

"Do you have food here?" I asked.

"I got a little something," he replied.

I got up to look in his fridge, and took out frozen shrimp, burrito shells, spinach, cheese, tomatoes, and hot sauce. I decided to make shrimp burritos, and bake some walnut chocolate chip cookies. I boiled some blueberry hot tea, then put it in a cold pitcher in the freezer to let it get cold while I cooked. I started cooking for myself when I was 12 years old, so by now I was like a damn gourmet chef. I could make a meal out of anything, unless I had absolutely nothing.

"It smells good in here. What did you find?" he asked, and kissed the back of my neck.

"Shrimp burritos, cookies, and iced tea," I replied.

"Damn ma. You need any help?" he asked, and I shook my head no. "Aight, well I'm gon' chill in the living room," he said.

Once I finished the food, we relaxed on his couch and stuffed our faces. I had never made shrimp burritos before, but they came out bomb as hell. The cookies were good too, and the tea came out better than I thought. After watching TV, we retired to the bedroom.

"Ooohhh, babe," I moaned as Julius sucked on my clit softly. I ran my fingers through his short, fade-like curls, as he plunged two fingers into me. "Julius. Ahhh," I whined as I came for the third time.

He laid on his back, and I straddled him. I put a hand on his chiseled abs, and slid down on his long, thick pole. I started to ride him nice and slow, just how he told me he liked.

"Damn, look at yo sexy ass," he moaned, with squinted eyes. He held onto my small waist, as I threw my head back to enjoy the feeling. "Look at me," he said. He loved for us to keep eye contact throughout sex.

I brought my head back up to stare his fine ass in the eyes.

"Ooohh, I'm cumming," I said as I bit my lip.

Julius flipped me on all fours, and entered me slowly from behind. He planted kisses down my spine, as he thrusted into me slowly. He bit my shoulder, making me moan loud as hell. He leaned back up, and then sped up his pace. The sound of us moaning, and him beating up my wetness was all you heard.

"I'm cumming Ju- ahhh," I moaned as I released all over his thick shaft.

"Cum on your dick ma," he commented as my body shivered. "Yes, just like that," he said, smacking and grabbing my ass.

He flipped me on my back, and slid into me slowly. *Damn he had a lot of stamina!* He cupped my small breast, and sucked my nipples. He switched from one to the other as he eased in and out of me.

"I love you Julius," I moaned as I felt another orgasm rising.

He sped up his pumps, and we both released together. He dipped his tongue in my mouth, leaving his dick still inside me. I was worried because he didn't say he-

"I love you too, Nat," he said in between kisses.

Nevermind!

Today, I had a meeting with my boss-man Hugo. He said he wanted to talk to me about some things, and I needed to talk to him as well. I needed to let him know that by the end of the year, I was moving to South Carolina.

For nine months now, I had been putting a plan in place to have my own drug ring. Working for Hugo was cool, but I wasn't the type of nigga to work for someone else my whole damn life.

I got a connect from Peru, and boy was it hard to do. I had to prove that I could move weight, and a lot of it. He gave me a nice amount of bricks at a discount, and I had to get them off as quickly as I could within the state I planned to move to - South Carolina. It wasn't hard for me to do, but when I'm working for Hugo at the same time here in Indiana, it made it difficult. What helped me some was the fact that I had my brother Rashad, and homie Tim help me out.

See, they didn't work for Hugo, but I would be sure to put them on when I moved to Charleston, South Carolina. Hugo, for some reason, only put Greg and I on. It was hard to get in with him, but these were my niggas and I knew they could do the job. They proved it to me by helping me move that weight from the Peruvian connect. The nigga was so impressed that he agreed to supply me only, in the whole state of South Carolina; yeah, he had a lot of faith in me. In my opinion, he had plenty reason to. I was a hard worker, and always made a way even when there wasn't one.

"What's up man?" I asked as I sat down across from Hugo.

"Making money as usual," he replied, and I nodded. "So you know you been doing a great job, and bringing me a lot of money," he started.

"I sure have," I said.

"Right, well I want to promote you," he smiled.

"Look man-"

"I want you to meet with a potential new connect. I need you to go to Los Angeles next month," he said matter-of-factly.

I hated when he just expected me to drop whatever the fuck I had going on to work. I felt like his assistant, and that was another reason I was dipping.

"Hugo, I need to talk to you. I plan on moving to South Carolina in December," I told him. I wasn't gon' tell him why, unless he asked. Ain't like I was scared of him, but I didn't want him to think I was using him.

"South Carolina? What's out there?" he asked.

"Work," I replied.

"Work?" he raised a brow until he finally understood. "Working for someone else, Julius? I thought I was good to you," he said.

"Nah, I got my own shit about pop off," I replied confidently. I may have been 20 years old, but I been in the game for six years. I felt more like I was 35.

"Your own shit? Wow. Well, meet with the connect please," he said. *What?*

"You still want me to assist you, even though I'm moving?" I asked.

"Yeah, I need to use all your services now, before you're gone," he laughed.

"Aight, well shoot me the details of the flight," I said.

This nigga had something up his sleeve. Why in the hell would you still want me to meet your connect, knowing I'm gon' have my own ring? Maybe he really trusted me, but in my head, I felt like he was on some other shit. I wasn't gon' stress it too much though, cause if he wanted to have beef, then so be it, but I wasn't about to stay in Indiana and work for nobody. I was taking my black ass to South Carolina to get way bigger money.

———

"So what that nigga say?" my boy Dash asked me. Dash was coming to Charleston as well. That man's trigger finger was something serious, and I needed him to come in case we had to put some niggas down–him and his brother Leese.

"He acted like everything was gravy, but I know it ain't," I replied, and sipped my beer.

"Ain't like you double crossing his ass. He can't expect you to want to work under him forever. He know you got too much ambition, and too many goals for that," my older brother Rashad commented, and shook his head.

"Exactly. I never took Hugo as a hater, so hopefully he really is cool about it-"

"But if not, we can handle ourselves. Ain't nobody scared of bruh," my homie Tim chimed in, and everyone nodded.

"Aye, anybody talked to Greg?" I asked.

"Nah, that nigga been ghost. Honestly, I think he and Bianca fucking around," Rashad said.

"I wouldn't be surprised, and that nigga wonder why he didn't get that invite to South Carolina," I said.

I could spot a snake anywhere and anytime, so I knew Greg wasn't that trustworthy. Yeah he was cool as a friend, or at least I thought, but when it came to doing business, I didn't fuck with him. My team consisted of my brother Rashad, Dash, Leese, Menzo, and Tim.

"What about Menzo? Where he at?" Rashad asked.

"That nigga at work," I chuckled. This nigga worked at Walmart, and was more than happy to make that move to Charleston when I brought it up. "Anyhow, everyone's flight is booked for November 30th, at 8 a.m.," I said.

"What you gon' do about Natalia?" Rashad asked.

"She coming too," I frowned.

"Does she know that? And ain't she gonna be in the middle of her senior year?" Tim asked.

"I'll tell her when I feel like it. I'm gon' see if she can take her GED or something though," I replied nodding, and so did everyone else. Natalia was *my* girl, and wherever I went, so did she, whether she wanted to or not.

"Well I can't wait, nigga! I'm ready to get this fucking bread!" Leese smiled, and raised his beer.

"Nigga!" I smiled, and everyone laughed.

NATALIA

Lucy, Victoria, and I were all at Denny's having dinner. Victoria was a co-worker of mine at CVS. We were gonna have a little girls night and relax. Lucy said she had some big news to tell me, and I couldn't wait to hear it.

"So what do you have to tell us?" I smiled.

"Dannngggg, can I order something to drink first?" Lucy chuckled.

As if the waitress heard her, she walked over to take our drink orders. Once she did, we went ahead and put in our food orders as well.

"Aight, come on!" Victoria said as soon as the waiter walked off.

"Welllll, I'm moving to South Carolina!" Lucy smiled.

"What? Why? Your mom got a new job?" I asked in disbelief.

"Nah, I'm going with my man –he's got a new job.," she smirked.

"Who is your man?" I asked, and Victoria laughed. Come on, we all knew Lucy got around. She had a new boo constantly.

"Menzo!" she replied, and rolled her eyes.

"Y'all that serious to where you moving to another state with him? South Carolina is a nice ways from here. Not like it's Illinois or Ohio," Victoria stated.

"Yes, we are super serious," Lucy smiled.

"What kind of work?" I asked.

"I don't know, but I know he finna be paid. He's gon' be working for Julius," Lucy nodded.

"Julius? Julius is moving to South Carolina?!" I frowned.

"Uh, yeah. I thought you knew!" Lucy frowned.

"I would've told you, don't you think?" I raised a brow.

"Well yes, Julius is moving. Him, his brother, Menzo, a couple other cats, and now me," she smiled.

I couldn't believe Julius was moving away and didn't say anything. Knowing him, he probably planned to just skip town and never speak to me again. I hated that I fell in love with him sometimes.

"When you moving?" Victoria asked.

"Our flight leaves at the very end of November," Lucy replied.

"What about senior year?" I inquired.

"Menzo brought up me taking my GED. So I'm just gon' do that and be done with that shit. School ain't about to hold me back from being with my man," Lucy replied.

"You don't want to experience senior year?" I frowned. I couldn't believe Lucy and Julius.

"Not really, for what? Prom? Please!" Lucy waved it off.

Me: You're moving?

I shot a text to Julius.

"Your mom cool with you skipping town?" Victoria asked.

"I ain't telling her. I'm gon' leave one morning, the morning of the flight, and never come back," Lucy replied.

We continued to talk until our food came. Once we finished eating, I cut our girls' night short, because I needed to go talk to Julius. He still hadn't responded to my text, and I needed to know what he was thinking.

JULIUS

I was tired as hell from working all damn day. I had been running the streets constantly to check on the traps Hugo had set up, as well as conducting business regarding my move to South Carolina. I was so excited to move over there, and start making more bread than I could count. I had just gotten a nice little condo out there, and was more than ready to go. In five months, I would be on my way. I just needed to tell Natalia.

I pulled into my driveway and exhaled heavily. All I wanted to do was shower and take my ass to bed. I was thinking of calling Natalia over, but I knew we'd be up all night, and I needed to be up bright and early.

TAP!

TAP!

TAP!

I looked over, and saw Daphne tapping on my passenger side window. I hit the unlock button, and she slid in.

"I missed you," she smiled.

"You saw me two days ago," I said non-chalantly.

"So, I can't get enough of you," she said, rubbing her hands over my crotch.

I shook my head, and pulled out my phone. I checked my notifications, as Daphne leaned down and took me into her mouth. She took in all eleven inches, and didn't gag as usual. I continued checking my texts as she went to work.

Baby Girl Nat: *You're moving?*

Me: *Come over so we can talk.*

I locked my phone up, and continued to enjoy Daphne slobbing me up. Natalia would be here in about 15 minutes, and my nut would be busted by then. Just as I felt my nut rising, I saw Natalia walking up to my door. *Fuck! Shit!*

"Get up!" I yelled to Daphne, and she sat up.

"What Julius?!" she frowned, wiping the spit from her mouth. Her eyes darted to Natalia at my door. "Wow, so you really claiming this bitch?"

"Shut the fuck up," I said as my phone started to ring. My ringtone was loud as hell, and Natalia followed it to my car. This was not happening right now.

TAP!

TAP!

TAP!

"Hey ma," I said, as I opened the door.

"Hi, Naomi?" Daphne played dumb.

"Julius, I need to talk to you abo-" Natalia stopped mid sentence, as her eyes locked onto my pelvis. *Fuck, forgot to zip my damn pants up.*

"Nat-" I tried grabbing her arm.

"No, let me go," she said calmly, as her eyes became glazed over.

I hopped out and jogged after her, but she was already in her car. I snatched open her passenger door, and got in while fixing my pants.

"Natalia let me explain," I said as tears ran down her face. "Daphne is just some hoe baby, you my girl," I said. She didn't respond; she only sniffled.

"I love you Julius, why do you have to treat me this way?" she cried.

"I love you too, Natalia," I said, and rubbed her hand. I grabbed it and kissed the back of it. I leaned over and kissed her soft lips. "I love you ma," I said in between kisses. I wiped her tears with my thumbs as they fell.

"Julius, I want to go home," she said.

"Fine, fuck it! Take your ass home!" I snatched the keys out the ignition. "But leave the fucking car so I can give it to my new bitch," I spat.

"Julius, it's 9 p.m.," she whined.

"You better start walking then," I frowned.

"Julius, I'm sorry. I-"

I hopped out the car and slammed the door. She got out as well, and I hit the alarm to lock the car. When I walked up, Daphne was at my door smiling at me. I took her in the house, fucked, and sent her home immediately. If Natalia couldn't get with the program, I'm sure there were plenty bitches in South Carolina that would.

I finally got home around 10:30 p.m., and I was exhausted. I couldn't believe Julius turned everything on me. I tried calling him a couple times, but he didn't answer once.

I walked into my apartment, and headed straight to the shower. As soon as I got out, I hurled all the contents of my stomach into the toilet. *God no,* I thought. I rinsed my mouth out, and drank a bottle of water. I looked at all the food in the fridge, knowing I needed to cherish it being there since Julius was done with me. I put a hot pocket in the microwave, and then went to brush my teeth. I ate my food, and then put a big t-shirt on to go to sleep. I thought about the pregnancy test that I had stolen from my job a while ago. I decided not to take it tonight, so I could sleep peacefully.

I woke up the next morning, and checked my phone. I still had no texts from Julius, and I saw some from Lucy, Victoria, and Frank. I replied to Lucy and Victoria, and then opened the one from Frank.

Frank: *You still taken? Come over.*

I didn't respond, and locked my phone. I got out of bed, and immediately felt my throat jump. I ran to the bathroom, and threw up violently. My stomach was in so much pain. I flushed it, then went to get the pregnancy test I had in my room. I walked it back to the bathroom, and let out a sigh of relief at the fact that my mother was still sleep. I cleaned my throw up off the toilet with some wipes, and then peed on the stick. As I waited, I saw the door was unlocked, so I quickly locked it.

After 5 minutes, I looked at the stick and saw the two deadly pink lines. I blew out hot air, then proceeded to brush my teeth and shower. I wrapped myself in a towel once I was done, grabbed the positive test, and then headed out the bathroom. I ran dead smack into my mother, and accidentally dropped the stick. She bent down and snatched it up before I could.

"I thought you wasn't fucking?" she said, and slapped the shit out of me.

"Wait let me-"

"Get the fuck out Natalia! Pack whatever you can, and go! I told you no damn babies!" she yelled as she rained blows on the back of my head and back.

"Okay! Okay!" I yelled, and sprinted to my room.

I stuffed as much as I could into my duffle bag, and then threw on some skinny jeans, a tube top, and flip-flops. My hair was still wet and curly, so I threw it up in a bun. I grabbed my phone to send some texts. *Where could I go?* Lucy's mom couldn't afford me.

Me: *Julius, I need you.*

I sent it, then grabbed my bag and left. I covered my ears as my mom called me all kinds of bitches and hoes for everyone to hear.

Me: *Julius please, I'm sorry.*

I waited outside my complex for half an hour, and still got no response from Julius. My phone buzzed, and I hurriedly pulled it out.

Frank: *You gon' come through or you still not fucking with me?*

Me: *Yeah. Come get me.*

I blew out hot air and bounced my leg nervously, as I waited for Frank's response.

Frank: *Almost there.*

I half smiled, hoping he would let me sleep on his couch at least. It was hot as hell, and I could really go for a cold water, but I had no way to get one right now. Ten minutes later, Frank pulled up and leaned over to open his passenger door. I jogged over, and then put my duffle bag in his back seat.

"Can I spend the night? Just for tonight, I have nowhere else to go," I said.

"Yeah ma, you lucky I got my own shit," he replied.

"Thank you," I smiled back.

He pulled off from the curb, and we headed towards his house. I was so happy when he decided to stop at Burger King, because I was starving and thirsty. I tried to pay for my own, but he stopped me. I was glad, because I had ordered a meal, plus a pie, which all came to $8. We pulled up to his apartment complex, and it was really nice. We walked through the door, and immediately sat down to eat.

"What do you do to be able to afford all this? You just graduated?" I frowned as I bit my burger.

"I have my ways," he smiled. He must've been a dope boy like Julius.

"I'm gonna to try to be out of your place ASAP," I said, sipping my strawberry soda.

"Don't trip ma, stay as long as you want. I been waiting to spend time with you for the longest," he smiled, and so did I. "So why you need to stay with me?" he asked.

"My sister and I had an argument," I said.

"She can just kick you out like that?" he frowned.

"It's her place," I replied.

"And what about old boy that snatched you out my whip?" he chuckled. "Why he not helping you? You his lady, right?" he raised a brow.

I shook my head no, as I balled up the burger paper.

"No, we are over," I smiled as if I didn't care, but deep down I was hurt. I was pregnant yet again, and Julius was MIA on me *yet again*, but this time I wasn't getting an abortion–whether he liked it or not.

"Damn, well maybe I have a chance," Frank smirked.

"Frank, I-I'd like that," I smiled. I was gonna tell him I was pregnant, but he may have kicked my ass out, and I didn't need that.

"Cool, cool," he nodded.

We watched TV, and talked for the rest of the night. I realized Frank wasn't as thirsty as I thought he was; he just really liked me. He didn't push up on me at all tonight, and I was happy. His apartment had two bedrooms, so he allowed me to stay in the other room.

"Unpack and make yourself comfortable," he said as he leaned in the doorway.

"Thank you. I will," I smiled, and he closed the door.

I unpacked my belongings, and then grabbed my shower gel to get clean. I stayed up all night listening to Tamia, and thinking about my horrible situation. This arrangement was not permanent, and I needed to figure out what I was gonna do.

NATALIA

I had been staying with Frank for a couple weeks now, with no texts or calls from Julius. As much as I tried to tell myself I didn't care, I did. I thought about him all day long. I didn't even want to watch anything that had to do with relationships, because it made me sad. I never saw him around the city, and it upset me even more.

My morning sickness had gotten worse, and I could barely keep my food down. Frank started to get suspicious, but I just told him I had a stomach bug. He wasn't no damn doctor, so he believed me.

Lucy Bff: Have fun tonight.

Me: Yeah right.

Tonight, or this evening, I was letting Frank take me out. It was the least I could do, since he'd taken me in for free. I wasn't used to watching TV, and using the house phone for free. I made sure to cook for him almost every night, so that I wouldn't feel too bad though. I also knew that him taking me out would keep my mind off Julius.

"You ready?" Frank peeked into my room.

He wore a black button up shirt, dark jeans, and Air Forces. His hair was freshly cut, and his cologne was intoxicating. I was slowly realizing I had a thing for guys who smelled good but as I said before, Frank was fine as hell.

"Ye-yeah I am," I slightly stammered, as I took in his flawless mocha complexion.

"Aight cool, you like Cheesecake Factory?" he asked, flashing his perfect smile.

"I'm not sure, I've never been," I shrugged.

"You haven't? What kind of nigga was you fucking with?" Frank frowned.

"Clearly not a good one," I smiled. I was talking a good game, but deep down Julius consumed my thoughts. It hurt to know he hadn't thought about me once.

"Well, hopefully we can change all that. And you look good as hell," he smiled, looking me up and down. I had on that same burgundy, sleeveless, turtleneck dress that I wore to Menzo's party awhile back. I wore some black sandals, and my hair was straightened, with a part down the middle.

"Thank you," I replied. Frank reached his arm out, and took my hand in his.

We listened to a bunch of different Problem songs the whole way there. Frank held my hand the whole way, and I can't say that I didn't like it. I was slightly paranoid that Julius would pop up like last time, but I knew that was slightly wishful thinking on my part; minus the little ass whooping he delivered. I just wanted to see him, regardless of the reason.

We arrived to Cheesecake Factory in no time, and I hoped there was something I would like. What the hell kind of restaurant is named after only dessert? I at least liked a hint on what you sold, like Red Lobster.

Frank hopped out, and opened my door. I smiled as he assisted me out, and we headed into the restaurant. We were seated immediately, because his homeboy was the hostess there. Thank God, cause my pregnant ass was starved.

"So what do you think so far?" Frank smiled.

I looked around the restaurant, and nodded my head. "It's cool, I judge by the food though," I chuckled.

"Well then you gon' love this place, especially when you taste the cheesecake." he winked. *Damn he was fine.*

"I hope so," I replied, opening the menu. "The cheapest thing is $15!" I yelped, surprised.

"You get what you pay for, ma. Get whatever you want though, this is date," Frank replied, looking over his menu.

I decided to get the Steak Diane and Salmon dish, because I hadn't had steak in so many years. I was hesitant on the salmon, but Frank assured me that it was good.

"This is probably the best strawberry lemonade, I've ever had," I smiled.

"Yeah, I think so too," he replied.

Our food arrived, and I was happy that I listened to Frank, because it was so damn good. Everything from the steak, to the potatoes, to the asparagus, and the salmon was bomb. I even ate the mushrooms, which I hated, that were mixed in with some sauce, and poured over the steak.

"You were so right about this, Frank," I beamed as I scooped same potatoes into my mouth.

"See, you gotta trust ya boy," he chuckled, and so did I.

"I'm happy you finally stopped playing me to the left, Natalia," he said.

"Me too. I just been dealing with a lot, I'm sorry," I replied.

"Nah, it's cool. I would've waited as long as I had to, just for this moment right here," he nodded. He grabbed my hand, and kissed the back of it.

We finished our meals, and then I got the cookie dough cheesecake to go. I wanted to eat it right then but since Frank said he was stuffed, I decided against it.

"Thank you for tonight Frank, I needed that," I said as we walked into his apartment.

"Me too," he said as he pulled me close.

He placed soft kisses on my neck, as his hands rubbed down my small back to touch my ass. I let out a soft moan as I melted in his embrace. He kissed up my neck, to my chin, and then my lips. His mouth felt so good against mine as we sucked each other's lips. We headed to the bedroom I slept in, and he laid me down on the bed.

"Wait Frank, I can't," I said, remembering the baby growing inside of me, and the love that I had for its father.

"What, why?" he asked out of breath. I opened and closed my mouth, looking for the words to say. "Don't do this Natalia, you know how I feel about you. We belong together ma," he said, kneeling down in front of me. He kissed my inner thighs, as his hands roamed up my dress. I closed my eyes and let out a soft moan as he kissed all the way up to my love box. He kissed the fabric of my panties, but it felt like I had none on.

"Frank, I can't," I said, pushing his head away. He threw his head back in irritation, and exhaled heavily. He stood up and placed his hands on his hips. "I'm sorry I-I just-"

"It's cool Natalia, you ain't ready. I can wait," he said. I nodded, because I couldn't tell him that I was pregnant by another guy. "Goodnight ma," he said as he kissed my forehead, and then walked out.

I fell back on my bed and sighed. I wish I had've dated Frank before Julius. He cared about me, and that's what I needed. Now I was 17 years old, and pregnant by and in love with a man who didn't give two shits about me; pregnant for the second time at that.

I finally got up, showered, and brushed my teeth. I turned on Aaliyah's Pandora station, and then drifted off to sleep. This couldn't be life.

Today was gon' be a good ass day for me. I hopped in my car, and rolled my window down all the way. I sped down the street, letting my hair blow in the wind. "All My Love" by Cassie blasted through my speakers, as I bobbed my head.

I know you wanna bad girl, give em all of that. Take his heart, won't give it back. I know you want all my love, give you all of that. I sang along with Cassie.

I finally arrived at my destination, with a huge ass smile on my face. I saw his car in the driveway, and text his phone.

Me: *I'm outside.*

Daddy Ju: *Come to the door.*

I locked my phone, and walked seductively up his walkway in case he was watching. I rang his doorbell, and after a couple seconds, he appeared. He had a scowl on his face, which made him all the sexier. He rocked an Indiana Pacers baseball jersey, jeans, and white lowtop forces. Damn.

"So what you have to show me?" he asked, obviously irritated by my presence. I didn't care because he would be mine again, in a matter of seconds.

"Well, I went out with my girl Daphne last night, and I saw your little boo," I smirked.

"I'm single," he spat, catching me off guard.

"You are?" I asked, and he nodded.

"You said you had something I needed to see?" he asked again. I didn't feel like I needed to show him now that he dumped Natalia, but just in case he thought about fucking with her again, I decided to.

"So I was out with Daphne, and I saw Natalia on a date with another dude. She was smiling and laughing and shit. She looked in love," I added on extras for my benefit.

"Yeah right. Natalia is on me, ain't no way she was out smiling all in some other nigga face already," he scoffed.

I pulled out my iPhone, and showed him the pictures. "Well it looks like she's over you."

I smiled when he snatched my phone from me. He feverishly scrolled through the many angles I took of them. I almost came, seeing how furious he became when he saw the picture of Natalia's new boo kissing her hand.

"Take this shit!" he spat. I had never seen Julius this mad, and it kind of hurt. I knew he would get upset, but I figured he'd shrug it off.

"They went to his apartment together too. She spent the night, and I think she's moved in with him. I followed her for a couple days, and everyday she gets off work, she goes to his apartment," I added as if I was trying to help. I was twerking on the inside; I was so happy.

"What?!" Julius snapped his neck towards me, and I swear I saw flames of fire in his dark brown eyes.

"Ye-yeah she-"

"What's this fuck nigga's address?!" he demanded. His nostrils flared, and he clenched his jaw.

I read off ole boy's address, as Julius typed it into his maps application. "Where you going?" I asked him as we stood up simultaneously.

"I'm about to snatch her ass up out this nigga's crib!" Julius yelled.

"Why? Fuck her! She obviously didn't love you like you thought! She's already moved on!" I pleaded.

"She don't move on until I say she can!" he yelled. I was taken aback by how angry he was over this little hoe.

"Julius, she isn't worth it baby. I'm the one that has loved you all this time. I haven't been with anyone since we broke up. She doesn't care about you!" I yelled.

"Oh and you do? How could you care about me if when my mama died you didn't even stop by? And don't think I don't know about you smashing Greg!" he yelled.

"I ain't never fucked Greg! And you and yo mama not even close, so miss me with tha-" before I could finish, Julius slapped the shit out of me.

"You watch yo fucking mouth when it comes to my mama, bitch! You don't know shit about how close we were!" he yelled, with his fists balled up.

"Julius, I'm sorry I jus-"

"Get the fuck out Bianca. Why you even looking out for me, hunh? Nothing you say or do will ever make me take yo ass back. Whether I'm with Natalia or not, I'm never gon' be with you again. You and I are a fuckin wrap ma! A fucking wrap!" he yelled, staring into my eyes.

He meant every word that had just come out of his mouth. I felt as if I was going to throw up. I can't believe I loved this man as much as I did.

"Well just to let you know, I am fucking Greg," I lied. I was way too in love with Julius to let another man touch me, but I wanted to hurt him with my words like he'd done me. In the back of my mind, I hoped he got as angry as he did when he saw those pictures of Natalia.

"And I been smashing Daphne for over a year, so we even," he replied calmly.

I frantically searched his eyes with mine, hoping I could see that he was lying like me. I didn't see anything of the sort, and next thing I knew tears were racing down my cheeks.

"You ain't shit Julius," I said with a trembling voice.

He nodded, and opened his front door for me to leave. I bit my lip hoping to stop the tears, only to realize it was sore and busted from his slap just moments ago. I stormed out and before I could turn around to speak, he slammed his door.

JULIUS

As soon as Bianca left, I headed to grab my gun and put it in my waist. I locked up my crib, then hopped in the whip. I mounted my iPhone, and let Siri lead me to this nigga that Natalia was playing house with. It was about 5 p.m. on a Saturday, so I knew Natalia would not be at work. *Perfect time to catch her in the act*, I thought. I swear on my mother's grave, if she was in there getting fucked, she was gon' die tonight, along with that nigga.

I pulled up at the complex, and parked my whip fast as hell. I didn't waste time straightening up my car up either. I looked down at my phone to check the apartment number, and raced over there to the door.

BOOM!

BOOM!

BOOM!

"Aye who the fuck is beating on my door?!" I heard a nigga yell. My blood boiled, and I felt as if it would burn through my skin. The door flung open, and it was that same nigga Natalia was in the car with that one night.

"Natalia!" I yelled as I barged my way in.

"Aye nigga, get the fuck out my shit!' the dude yelled, following after me.

"Back the fuck up homie," I said through gritted teeth. I pulled my gun from my waist, and pointed it in his direction.

"Julius!" I heard Natalia yelp.

"Get your shit and come on!" I yelled to her.

"Okay, okay. Just don't sho-"

"Hurry the fuck up, Natalia!" I boomed.

I directed my attention back to her little side nigga, as he stood there with his hands up. I looked around the apartment, and saw he was living okay.

"You better not have fucked my bitch," I glared at him.

"Well, according to her, y'all are broken up," he smirked. I cocked my gun, and his smirk immediately faded.

"I'm ready." Natalia finally appeared back into the living room, with her duffle bag and phone.

"Let's go," I said, pushing her towards the door. "If I catch you around her again, I'm pulling the trigger." He nodded and smiled, like I was bullshitting. I wanted so badly to shoot his ass, but I wasn't reckless. I was gon' give him one more chance to stop sniffing around Natalia. I walked out, and put my gun away.

Once we reached my car, I snatched Natalia's bag off her shoulder. I threw it in the backseat, and then jogged to my side.

"Get in!" I yelled, and she did as I asked.

The whole way to my house, she stared out the window as tears flowed freely down her face. I finally pulled up to my crib, and we both got out the car. I grabbed her bag roughly, and we headed into the house. Once we got in, she tried to walk to the bathroom, but I grabbed her arm.

"You fuck that nigga?" I asked.

"Why does it matter? You haven't talked to me in a month," she cried.

"I'm gon' ask your ass one more time, and you better be honest," I said, tightening my grip.

"Ow, Julius!" she cried, only pissing me off more.

I slapped her ass hard as hell, and she fell onto the couch. She hopped up to run, but I grabbed her by the waist and flung her onto the couch. I grabbed her by her hair, and bent her head back.

"Did you fuck him?!" I yelled as she cried hard as hell.

"N-no I didn't," she stammered.

"You a got damn lie!" I yelled. I let her hair go, and turned to the kitchen.

"I'm not lying!" she yelled, and stood up. Her bottom row of teeth was covered in blood.

I backhanded her again, as visions of her fucking that nigga flooded my mind. She flew into the nearby wall, and slid down it crying. I lifted her up by her hair, and prepared to deck her already bloody face.

"Please, Julius, I'm pregnant!" she whimpered.

"You got pregnant by that nigga?!" I yelled.

"I haven't fucked him! This is your baby! Just like the last one!" she yelled as tears soaked her cheeks. I stood there staring at her, breathing hard as hell. "You can't put your hands on me Julius, I thought you loved me," she continued to cry hard as hell. Suddenly, she ran to the bathroom to throw up violently. Once she was done, she dropped her head in her hands, to cry some more. "I thought you loved me," she cried, almost to herself. Her body appeared to be dry heaving as she sobbed.

I stood her up, and removed her clothes. She continued to cry as if I wasn't there, and I turned on the bath water. I picked her up, and placed her into the warm bath, and by now she was only sniffling. I grabbed a warm towel, and dabbed her bloody face. *What the fuck did I do?* She winced in pain, as I cleaned her wounds. I kissed her cheek, and she slightly moved a way. I left out the bathroom to look through her bag for her soap. I knew it was her favorite. Once I located her Herbal Essence body wash, I went back to the bathroom. I bathed her body, and we didn't say anything to one another. Once she was clean, I picked her up out the tub and took her to my room to dry her off. I gave her a big t-shirt to put on, and then went to Subway.

"I got you something to eat baby girl," I said as I walked into the bedroom.

"Thank you," she replied slightly above a whisper, as she sat up on the bed.

"I'm sorry baby. I was just so angry, thinking you was in love with another nigga. Are you?" I asked, sitting down next to her.

"No Julius, how many times do I have to tell you that I love you," she replied as she stared at her food.

"Why was you with him?" I asked.

"My mom kicked me out. I called and text you, but as usual you ignored me. I had nowhere else to go, and he cared about me enough to answer so..." she shrugged and bit her sandwich.

"Natalia, I'm sorry babe. You know I love you."

"No I don't know. You treat me like shit 24/7," she started to cry again. It was a silent cry, and her tears fell from her eyes onto the subway paper.

"I know ma, but that shit is gon' stop ASAP. I love you and I don't want you thinking otherwise, aight?" I asked, and she was silent. I put my sandwich to the side, and scooted closer to her. "Aight?" I asked again, and she nodded.

I moved her sandwich out of her lap, then grabbed her around the waist and leaned her back. I kissed her soft lips, as I laid between her soft legs.

"I missed you ma," I said in between kisses. Her lip was slightly swollen, and I felt like shit. I kissed the tears that ran down her beautiful face, and removed her shirt.

"I missed you too, Julius. But I'm keeping my baby," she replied, looking me in the eyes.

"You mean you're keeping *our* baby," I smiled, and I could tell she was surprised.

"I love you Julius," she said as more tears escaped her beautiful brown eyes. I entered her slowly, and she let out a soft moan into my mouth.

"I love you too, Natalia," I replied in between kisses. "Your shit is the best, baby," I moaned.

"Ahh, Oohh, Julius," she moaned as she released on my dick.

I exploded into her in no time, and we kissed for what seemed like an hour straight. I planted kisses down her body, until I reached her stomach. I gave a couple extra soft kisses, knowing my baby was in there.

"You're moving to South Carolina?" she asked as I trailed kisses along her inner thigh.

"Yeah, you and I," I replied, still kissing my way up.

"How? I have a year left of school."

"You can get your GED like Lucy," I replied, nearing her pretty pussy.

"Julius I ca- oohhh ahhhh," she moaned as I pulled her clit into my mouth.

"You can't what?" I asked in between making love to her pussy with my mouth.

"Ahhh, oh my go- ahhh," she moaned as she arched her back.

I continued sucking and licking until she exploded. Her body shivered, as she let out soft moans every now and then.

"You moving with me, aight?" I asked as I kissed on her lips. She shook her head yes, and wrapped her arms around my neck. "Now get some sleep, cause we going to Los Angeles tomorrow," I added.

"We are? Why? I don't have good clothes."

"I got some business to take care of, but I want to make some things up to you. Cheating on you and putting my hands on you," I replied. "Plus, we can go shopping if you feel your clothes aren't good enough."

She paused for a moment, to caress my face. "You're lucky I'm on summer break," she smiled.

"No *you* lucky you on summer break," I said, kissing her lips.

She laid on my chest, and we talked until she fell asleep.

NATALIA

I t was Sunday afternoon when we arrived to LAX airport, in Los Angeles, California. I had never been on a plane before, so it was a little scary. I had the window seat, but Julius willingly switched with me. The people working on the plane were really nice, and Julius said it was because we were in first class. I don't really know what the hell that means, but I enjoyed it nonetheless. We had a nice breakfast, tea, and juice.

I only had my same duffle bag, so we grabbed that and Julius' luggage before heading outside to look for a taxi. Once we got one, we hopped in and headed to our hotel room.

We arrived to the Four Seasons in Los Angeles, and I was in awe due to the outside of the place. It was tall as hell, and reminded me of the movies. Julius paid the taxi driver, and we hopped out to go inside. The lobby area looked like one of a huge mansion. Julius grabbed my hand to go check into the room, snapping me out of my admiration. Once we did, we headed up to the room and it was beautiful. It looked like an apartment. When I hear hotel room, I expect a room, but this was a full on living quarter.

"This is so nice," I said a little above a whisper.

"I know right," Julius replied as he sat our bags down.

"How long are we here?"

"7 days, one whole week," he smiled.

Me: This hotel is so nice.

Lucy Bff: Send pictures!!

I walked around the miniature apartment for a little bit, to take a couple pictures for Lucy. I wasn't really used to places this nice. The last nice place I stayed at was Julius' house, and it wasn't even a mansion or anything.

"I wanted to take you to dinner tonight, ma," Julius said, breaking me from my thoughts.

"Where to?" I asked.

"It's a surprise. But where have you always wanted to go?"

"Lucille's BBQ," I replied.

"You know there is a Lucille's in Indiana, right?" he asked.

"Yeah, two hours away from us!" I smiled.

"Aight, well...I guess we can go there. Let's take a shower and go shopping first though," he said, walking over to me and kissing my lips.

He picked me up, and I wrapped my legs around his waist. We kissed passionately, until we reached the huge ass bathroom. I squirmed a little, so Julius could put me down. Once he did, I inspected the beautiful bathroom, with marble floors and counter tops. The shower had glass doors, and there was the biggest mirror I had ever seen along the wall.

"I never want to leave," I smiled.

"Trust me ma, once I start bringing in more cash in Charleston, this is gon' be small potatoes," Julius smiled as he admired the bathroom as well.

I got on my tiptoes to kiss his soft lips, and then we started to undress. His body was perfect, especially his flawless caramel complexion. There wasn't an imperfection in sight, from head to toe.

"I love your body babe," Julius said.

I guess I hadn't realized he was staring at me, just as I was staring at him. I pulled my long brown hair out of its ponytail holder as he neared me with a lustful stare. He kissed my lips, and then went to turn on the water for our shower. Once I stepped in with him, he picked me up in his strong arms, and we kissed as the showerhead wet our bodies. He was so strong, and I felt like a feather in his arms. He sat me on the shower seat, and put my legs on his shoulders. He kissed my lower lips softly and slowly, making me go crazy with anticipation.

"I love you Julius," I moaned, knowing what was about to come.

Julius took my clit into his mouth, and licked and sucked it gently. He slightly lifted my legs off his shoulders some in order to get more access. I grabbed onto the handle bar in the shower to make sure I didn't slip as he took me there.

"Ahhh, ooohhh, ahhhh," I moaned as I took my other hand to run my fingers through his soft, short fade.

He continued to make love to my pussy, and I was cumming in no time. He lapped it up, and continued working his magic on me. My body started to shake, and I felt as if I was gonna fall. It felt so good; I felt as if I couldn't control my trembling legs and torso. I exploded again, and he kissed my lower lips softly, while licking between the slit here and there.

"Get away," I moaned as I lightly pushed his head.

"Can't take no more," he chuckled as he stood up.

He towered over me, and dipped his tongue in my mouth. He grabbed a handful of my hair, and leaned my head back. He sucked and kissed on my neck, then down to my hard nipples. They were sore, I guess from me being pregnant, but the pain was even still pleasurable. He kissed back up to my lips, and I dropped down to my knees.

"Sloppy daddy?" I asked, already knowing the answer.

"You already know," he smiled.

I took him into my mouth, and let my saliva do its own thing. Lucy told me to not try to control my saliva, and let it just flow. His dick was covered in it as I bobbed up and down on his eleven inches. I took his balls into my hand, and massaged them slowly as I kept my rhythm with his dick.

"Natalia, fuck. Ahhh, shit."

I smiled, because Lucy said if he cursed, that meant I was doing a good job. His moans and obscene language gave me more ammo to go harder in the paint. I sped up and slowed down, then sucked on the tip.

"Ah, ahh fuck!" Julius moaned, and I looked up a little to make sure he was okay.

I'd never heard him talk or moan in such a high pitch. His right hand was pressed against the shower wall, as he threw his head back.

"Shit, ma, ahhh, I'm bout to nut," he moaned, sounding like he was about to have an asthma attack.

He stared down at me, and grabbed a fistful of my hair. He slowly wound his hips into my mouth, and I took every stroke no matter how far he went. Lucy's little class using big stick popsicles really helped.

"Fuck. Fuck," he moaned as I felt a warm liquid spill down my throat. I bobbed down once more, and cleaned it all off his dick. Once I got to the tip, I sucked softly but strongly. "Nat, ahh, oh," he whimpered like a little kitten.

As soon as I stood up, he rushed me into the wall and tongued me down. He licked on my neck and collarbone, and then lifted me up in the air. I wrapped my legs around his waist, as I let his thick dick fill me up. I wrapped my arms around his strong biceps and back, as he plowed into me at a perfect pace.

"Ahhh Julius, I'm cumming."

"Me too ma, fuck. Why is this pussy so good?" he asked no one in particular.

The sound of our wet skin smacking together and our moans was like music to my ears. Right as I came on his dick, he exploded into me. We kissed for a couple minutes, in the same position, before he finally let me down. We bathed, and then exited the shower to get ready for the first part of our day.

"Natalia, that was hands down the best head I've ever gotten ma," Julius said as he looked over his short, curly fade in the big bathroom mirror. His towel was wrapped around his waist, and his strong back, chest, and perfect abs glistened.

"Good, I don't want you going nowhere else for it," I said as I neared him for a hug.

"Nah, you wifey. You know that. I'm all about you, baby girl," he said, looking down into my eyes.

"You promise?" I asked sincerely.

"I promise, I'm gon' make you my wife one day. Especially now that I know how good you can suck a nigga up. That pussy and that mouth is mine," he smirked, with his fine ass. He dropped down and kissed my stomach, then headed out to finish dressing.

I smiled after hearing he was serious about me. I never thought I'd hear Julius say he loved me, *and* that he planned to make me his wife. We were only 17 and 20, so I knew it wouldn't be for a while, but still. This was the man that I loved more than anything, and to know he felt the same made me all giddy inside.

Once we were dressed, we went shopping at the Beverly Hills mall, or the Beverly Center as Julius called it. Everything in this mall was expensive as hell, but I guess these Californians were used to it. Back in Indiana, anything more than $40 was expensive as hell to me.

Our first stop was at Bath and Body Works, where I got a whole bunch of candles and wallflowers. I'd never seen anything like them, but when the employee explained how they worked, I had to have some. I've always been obsessed with candles, so I got about 15 of those. After that, it was Bebe, Dolce and Gabbana, Guess, BCBG, Jimmy Choo, Bloomingdales, Foot Locker, Louis Vuitton, Aldo, and Victoria's Secret, where I was finally able to get something sexy to wear for Julius.

He laughed at me, because every time the associate would tell us the total, I always looked worried. We also decided to stop by Armani to get Julius some more business professional clothing. He said he needed to be more professional, since he was gonna be a boss man when we got to South Carolina. After we stopped at Apple to get me a laptop and iPad, we headed back to the hotel to get dressed for dinner.

"Julius I can't believe you bought me all this stuff," I said as I spread the bags around the room.

"This was nothing, wait until I start making some real money," he chuckled as he sat in the chair.

"Well this is good enough for me. How are we gonna get all this back to Indiana?"

"My boss is sending his private jet to pick us up. He was using it the day we left, so that's why we couldn't have it then," he said, sipping some sparkling water.

I stood up off the bed, and walked over to him. I sat in his lap, and wrapped my arms around his shoulders.

"What?" he smiled.

"I want you to know that, even without all this, I would still be in love with you," I said.

"I hope so," he chuckled. "But nah, I know ma. You still loved me after all this time, when I treated you like shit so…" he shrugged, and I nodded. "But let's get dressed for dinner, I wanted to take you somewhere special tonight, and then tomorrow after a day of pampering, we can go to Lucille's," he offered.

"That's fine," I replied.

After talking for a little bit more, we went ahead and took a bubble bath together. He was upset once he realized I used one of my Bath and Body Works bubble baths, but I convinced him the scent wouldn't stick. After our sensual bath, we brushed our teeth and proceeded to get dressed. I decided to go with the new dress I got from Guess. It was an all-white sleeveless fringe dress, with sheer material around my collarbone and upper back. I paired it with some all-white sandal stilettos that I got from Aldo. I pinned my curly brown hair into a messy bun, and let a few small short curls hang by my temples and the nape of my neck. I spiced it up with a red lipstick that I got from MAC while in Bloomingdales. I made sure to get all the stuff I wanted to try from watching those makeup gurus on YouTube.

Once I was dressed, I looked over and saw Julius all dressed up. He wore a black button up, with a navy blue tux on top, courtesy of Armani. His wrist bore an iced out watch that literally blinded me when I looked at it. He wore an iced out chain to match that wasn't too big or too small. It was finished off with all-black dress shoes, whose brand I wasn't sure of.

"You look beautiful, Nat," he commented as he eyed my body. He bit his lip and smiled at me seductively. "If you wasn't already pregnant, I'd def be getting you pregnant tonight," he smiled.

He walked over to me, and his Dolce and Gabbana cologne filled the air. He wrapped his strong arms around my small waist, and leaned down to kiss me. I gave him a light peck, not wanting to mess up my lipstick.

"Aight, let's be out," he said as he walked over and opened the hotel room door for me. I grabbed my small white purse, and walked out.

When we got down to the lobby, we headed outside to see a driver waiting by a Bentley.

"Mr. Tate," he smiled and opened the door. We climbed in, and the driver jogged around to take us to our destination. The drive seemed to be pretty long, but I didn't mind because we were having good conversation. We pulled into a shopping center with a coffee bean and CVS, to eat at a restaurant named Houston's.

"I've never heard of this place," I said, looking at the beautiful architecture.

"I have a couple times, when I had to come out here before," he said, looking on with me.

"You brought Bianca?" I asked.

"What? Hell nah!" he chuckled. "Bianca and I have never been outside of Indianapolis," he laughed, as if my question was a joke.

The driver pulled up in front of the restaurant, and let us out. We walked in, hand in hand, and Julius gave the waiter his name. We were seated immediately since he had a reservation I guess. After we were seated, a waitress came over to take our drink orders and since we were ready, she jotted down the food as well.

"So how did you get that Bentley to come?" I asked. We were sitting in one of those rounded booths, so Julius and I sat at the center of it in order to be right next to one another.

"Dinero, ma. Everything costs money these days," he nodded.

"Your boss is nice to allow us to ride the jet home," I said.

"Yeah, makes me feel a bit bad about leaving him to go to Charleston."

"Why are you going?"

"I ain't never been the type of nigga to work for nobody. I've always wanted to have my own shit. That's why I could never hold down a regular job and shit. I wasn't too keen on a muthafucka telling me what to do," he replied, with squinted eyes like he was thinking.

"Yeah, I could only imagine working for myself."

"Yeah I'm ready, I been planning this move and getting everything in order for almost a year. I guess you could say I'm a perfectionist when it comes to business," he chuckled.

"You're a perfectionist when it comes to other things too," I replied.

"Oh yeah? Like what?"

"Like being a great boyfriend. When you really care about something, you do it perfect," I said cupping his face and staring into his eyes.

"Damn, I never saw it like that, but you're right. You the first girl I can say I cared about, and maybe that's why you got me acting like this. I usually don't do and say all this romantic shit," he chuckled lightly.

"You've never taken Bianca or any girl on a date?" I asked.

"I mean, I took her out to eat and shit, but dressing up, exchanging I love you's, and having meaningful conversations like this, was never on the menu; no pun intended," he smiled, and I laughed.

"Well I can't say I'm disappointed to hear that," I smiled, and so did he.

We shared a couple pecks, and our dinner came about ten minutes later. I finished all of mine, I guess because of the baby. We ordered and ate dessert, and I had a good time obviously.

"You know I'd never been on a date until you took me to Olive Garden that time," I said as we rode to the beach to relax.

"That's crazy. None of them knuckleheads at school asked?"

"Yeah, but I always said no."

"Damn, so big daddy made you say yes?" he laughed.

"Whatever," I smiled.

We spent a couple hours at the beach, just walking through the sand and talking. I got to know my love way more than I thought I ever could. After the beach, the driver took us back to the hotel, where Julius somehow a bottle of champagne on ice waiting. He said it was called Dom Per-something. All I knew was that it was in the prettiest white gold bottle. I couldn't drink any, so I wondered why he got it.

"How much you think this shit cost?" he asked as he laid across the floor sipping it.

"Is it expensive?" I asked and he nodded. "Okay, $200?" I asked, and he shook his head laughing. "Higher or lower?" I asked, and he pointed up in the air. "Mmmmm $500?" I asked, looking over the bottle.

"Almost $2500 ma," he replied.

"I would never spend that much on champagne!" I bucked my eyes.

"Me either, my boss bought this bullshit," we laughed in unison.

He killed the whole bottle off, as we sat and talked some more. We talked about our families, especially our mothers. I told him how my mother had made me act as if she was my sister since I was 4 years old. He told me how his mother was the prototype, until she met a guy who got her hooked on drugs. It made me worry about my mother, cause she dated all kinds of guys. Dalia and I didn't get along much, but I would still hate for something to happen to her.

After good convo, we made love for hours. Sex with drunk Julius was much different than with sober Julius. It was still phenomenal, but he was a little freakier. He ate me out for about 20 damn minutes, and had me weak as hell. He was licking and sucking from my anal cavity, all the way to my belly button. I was spent.

JULIUS

While Natalia was being pampered, it was time for me to go have this meeting with Hugo's potential connect. This the type of shit I be talking about. I have no problem meeting with a connect, but for some reason I feel like his little errand boy. I know he sent me on these out of town trips because he trusted me the most, but it just didn't feel like that. It didn't matter what I had going on, he wanted me to drop everything and go.

I threw on blue jeans, a light blue button up, and a black casual blazer. I threw on some all black chucks to complete my look, sprayed my cologne, and then headed out. I decided to go business casual, that way I didn't have to worry about being too dressed up or too dressed down.

That Bentley ride was only for last night, so today I took a taxi. The connect said he was staying at the Sheraton, so it wasn't too far from where I was already staying. Like I assumed, the taxi pulled up in no time. I paid my fee, and then headed inside. The lobby area was off the damn chain, and I made a mental note to stay here when I was footing the bill. I lowkey felt like Hugo should've had Natalia and I up in this shit. Then again, I was here to do business, not vacation; in his eyes, at least.

I asked the employee where the lobby bar was and once I found it, I decided to take a seat since I didn't see him. Hugo said the connect knew what I looked like, and that was all he could tell me. *What kind of shit is that?* I was used to Hugo's bullshit by now though. I decided to check a couple of texts, while I waited.

Franceska: Where you been? I dropped by yesterday.

Me: Handling business out of town.

Franceska: I miss you, can I see you when you get back?

Me: I don't know ma. I'm tryna stay faithful right now.

Franceska: You know I won't say shit Ju, I'm not even like that!

Me: Aight, I'll get at you when I get back ma

Franceska: Okay baby, I love you.

I shook my head, and locked my phone. I honestly don't know what I did to make all these bitches fall in love. Natalia was literally the only woman I gave any kind of extra attention to. I dicked these hoes down and then barely answered their calls, but somehow by our next convo they were in love. Franceska was some Dominican chick I met while out with my boys one night. She was sexy as hell, and I knew immediately that I was gon' fuck.

"Julius?"

I turned around to see a short, fat, black man. He appeared to be about 55 years old, and smelled like money. You know them colognes old niggas with money wear. It don't smell good, nor does it stink, it just says…money.

"That's me," I responded, and stood up.

He smiled and reached his hand out for me to shake it. I was a little confused, because Hugo said the guy didn't know my name. He said he just described him to me, and then for me to let him know what I was wearing.

"Pleasure to meet you, young man," he said as he slid into his seat across from me. "Would you like a drink?" he asked as he waived a waitress over.

"I'm not exactly of age," I replied.

"Nonsense," he replied, and turned to the waitress. "I will have a uh, vodka tonic and…?" he said, looking at me.

"I will take a scotch on the rocks," I half smiled at the waitress.

She wrote my drink down, and ran her tongue over her perfect teeth. She tucked her bob behind her ears, "Anything else for you two?" she asked, only looking at me.

"That'll be all darling," the connect replied, and I nodded in agreement. She smiled, then switched off. "Looks like some for sure pussy for you tonight," he joked.

"Uh, nah. But I didn't catch your name," I said.

"Forgive me, you can call me Bart," he smiled.

"I can *call you* Bart?"

"Mother named me Bartholomew."

"I see," we chuckled in unison.

"So Julius, Hugo sent you to meet with me about me becoming a possible connect. Did he like, give a questionnaire of some sort," he laughed, and so did I.

"Uh, no. I-I ask all the appropriate questions myself," I nodded as the waitress sat down our drinks.

I saw she had written her name and number on the napkin. When I looked up, she winked at me, bit her lip, and then walked away. She was beautiful as hell, with her blemish free mocha complexion, curvy body, and full lips. I was trying to do right by my baby girl, but boy was it hard.

"Nice. Nice. So go ahead I guess," Bart said, sipping his drink.

"Well first, how did you know my name?"

He paused and chuckled. "Besides the fact that I know everything about pretty much everyone, I heard about you from another connect in the business. He got drunk, and was bragging about a new partnership he got with a Julius Tate, and how much money you brought him on a trial run in a state you didn't even live in yet. So I did some digging, and I saw you worked for Hugo, and told him to send you to meet me," he smiled.

"Wait, so you requested that I come?" I frowned, and he nodded. "Why?"

"Fuck Hugo, I want to do business with you," he said.

"But I have a connect, as you know, and he lives closer to where I'm moving, actually right in South Carolina."

"So do I! How do you think he and I ended up at the same party together?" he laughed. "I'm just out here with my wife and daughters on a small vacation," he winked.

"Wait let me get this straight. You heard about me, you did some digging, saw I worked for Hugo, and then had me fly out here in hopes of becoming a connect for me and not Hugo?" I frowned, and he nodded the whole time I talked. I pinched the bridge of my nose, and let out a sigh. "This is crazy."

"So what do you say? My cocaine is pure and straight from Peru," he said smiling.

"So is my current connect's shit."

"They're the same, but not," he replied.

"What?" I frowned.

"You've heard of Coffee Bean and Starbucks right?" he asked and I nodded, trying to see where the fuck he was going with this. "So they are both coffee shops, which specialize in handcrafted drinks. However, Starbucks is the Michael Jackson of that shit. Buy a coffee drink from Coffee Bean, and then buy that same one from Starbucks, and you will see how watered down Coffee Bean's is. Now if you want them coffee bean bricks, by all means continue with the connect you have. But if you really want to dominate this fucking game, if you really want to fuck everybody else's shit up, including Hugo's, you'll fuck with Starbucks," he said, staring me in the eyes.

. . .

I knew he wasn't on no bullshit; however, I was a nigga that worked off loyalty. It didn't feel right to end shit with my potential connect, and then *also* snatch the rug from under Hugo.

"I can't do that to Hugo, man," I replied defeated.

"I mean, either way he's gon' be mad at you."

"Why is that?"

"Because he's not getting me as a connect. Most of the money he makes is from you pushing his weight. If he loses you, I'm sure the money will dwindle, and I'll be damned if he lowers his shipment amount on me," he said waving, letting the little waiter know we wanted drink refills. I didn't even realize that I had finished mine as well.

"So what you saying is, when I head back to Indiana, either I can head back with an A1 connect, or without one. But either way, Hugo is gon' be somewhat off me," I said, and looked out the huge window of the lobby.

. . .

Shit, if Hugo wasn't gon' get the connect, then why couldn't I? What's the point of wasting a good ass connect?

"So what do you say, Mr. Julius? Do you wanna make some real fucking money and take over? The streets in Charleston are dry as hell right now. I know you knew that, cause you smart and you loyal. You'd rather work your way up in an unfamiliar place, than step on the toes of those that have been good to you. That's the kind of muthafuckas I want to work with," he said.

"I need to think, I can't do Hugo like that," I said, shaking my head.

Bart held up one finger, as he pulled out his Blackberry. He started dialing on it, and then showed me the number he was dialing. I saw it was Hugo's, and mouthed *okay?* The phone started to ring, and I could hear clearly, although it was a little party going on around us.

"Bart, my man!" Hugo boomed through. Bart put a finger up to his mouth, to tell me to be quiet.

"Hey Hugo man, I'm not sure if our little deal is gonna work," Bart said.

. . .

"**W**hat? Why? You've met with my worker already?" he asked. *Worker? Get the fuck outta here*, I thought.

"**Y**es, yes I have, and that's the problem. I didn't mesh well with him, and if you want to work with me, you need to get rid of him," Bart said, smiling at me. *What was going on?*

"**D**one," Hugo replied, and surprised the fuck out of me.

"**G**reat, well let me know when you let him go, and call me back," Bart said.

"**G**ot you," Hugo said, and they disconnected.

"**N**ow you see, some people don't deserve such loyalty, such as him. He didn't even try to fight for you," Bart said, putting his Blackberry away.

I shook my head as the waitress brought over our refilled drinks. I raised mine in the air, "To getting this fucking money," I said.

. . .

"Hell yeah!" Bart laughed as we clinked glasses.

"Now Bart, my nigga, all the money you got and you rocking a Blackberry?" I smiled.

"Look I can't get into all that touchscreen shit! I'm old school, I'd take a 2-way if they had it!" he said, and we laughed in unison.

I stayed and mingled for a while, meeting with a couple people, including Bart's wife and daughters. His daughter Skylar was definitely on me, but I was not tryna go there with her. It was 8 p.m., so I decided to head to the hotel so I could be with Natalia. As I was walking out, that same waitress stopped me.

"You left your napkin," she smiled.

"I know," I chuckled.

"You should at least store it in your phone. You may need it one day, I'm that bitch you want to wife," she smiled.

. . .

"Oh you are?" I raised a brow.

"I am, sexy."

"Well unfortunately..." I stopped to look at her name on the napkin. "Unfortunately Emily, I have a *"wifey,"* and I think I have enough chicks waiting in line on the side," I replied.

"Well I plan to get VIP access over that line," she said.

"Doubt it ma," I shrugged, and my phone chimed. I looked at it, and saw it was Natalia.

"Is that her?" she asked.

"Yep," I said as I walked off, dropping the napkin. I had enough women tryna get on and I definitely didn't need another.

"Baby girl. Why you not dressed?" I asked Natalia as I walked into our hotel suite.

"I'm sick," she pouted.

I walked over and took my blazer and shoes off before climbing into bed with her. I could tell she just got out the shower, cause her long hair was a bit damp. She had on a red bra and red panties. She looked so sexy, and she wasn't even dressed.

"What you mean you sick? You got a cold?" I asked, getting off the bed and undressing down to my boxers.

"No, stomach ache. The baby is really making me sick," she half smiled.

I pulled the covers back, and climbed in bed with her. I pulled her close and started kissing her face. I got between her legs, and pinned her hands above her head as I dipped my tongue in her mouth. I kissed from her soft lips to her chin, down to her small, perky breasts. I reached under her to unsnap her bra, and she stopped me.

. . .

"What's wrong?" I asked.

"I'm not feeling well, Julius," she replied, looking up at me in the eyes.

"Just lay there," I said as I started to kiss down her stomach.

"No, and I'm hungry," she whined as she pushed my head away. *Fuck.* My dick was rock hard. "Can you get me some food?"

"What you want?" I asked, getting out of the bed.

"A chicken nugget meal from McDonalds, and then some vanilla ice cream to dip the fries in," she said smiling.

I shook my head and kissed her soft lips.

· · ·

"Fries and ice cream, ma?"

"Yeah, I just thought of it and it sounds good."

"Aight, I'll be back in a bit," I said, throwing on some basketball shorts and a t-shirt. I threw on my Jordan 3's, then my snapback.

I grabbed the room key, my phone, and then left out. I couldn't believe I wasn't getting no pussy tonight, and that I was out running errands in a damn taxi. Once I got in the taxi, my phone buzzed with an unknown number.

"Can you take me to the nearest McDonalds, preferably one that's near a grocery store," I told the driver as I pulled my phone out.

(843) 555-5555: *Hey sexy.*

M*e: ?*

. . .

(843) 555-5555: It's Emily.

Me: How you get my number?

This bitch already had stalker tendencies.

(843) 555 -5555: Mr. Vargas

Me: Who?

(843) 555-5555: Bart nigga. lol.

I locked my phone once we pulled up to Ralphs. "Aye man, wait here and I'm gon' come back so we can hit Mickey D's," I said.

. . .

"No you pay first!" the driver spat.

I paid him for the ride, then ran into get some vanilla ice cream. I rushed, cause I was hoping his ass didn't leave. I breathed a sigh of relief once I came out and saw he was still waiting for me. We stopped by McDonalds for Natalia's food, and then headed back to the hotel.

As I walked onto the elevator, my phone buzzed again. I pulled it out and exhaled heavily.

(843) 555-5555: No response? Anyway, I'm tryna see you tonight.

Me: For what?

(843) 555-5555: To chill.

Me: I got a girl that I can chill with.

. . .

(8

43) 555-555: Damn, well we can smoke and fuck.

Me: Cool, send your location.

"I got your food greedy," I smiled when I walked into the hotel room.

"Thank you baby. I'm sorry," Natalia replied.

"Sorry for what?"

"That I didn't want to do it tonight," she said.

"You change your mind?" I asked.

. . .

"No, maybe tomorrow. I feel too si-"

"Aight, well I'll be back in a little bit," I said, cutting her off and leaving.

My phone buzzed, and I saw Emily had text me her room number. She was at the Sheraton, the same hotel as Bart, so I knew how to get there. These taxis were making a damn killing off my ass.

I arrived back at the Sheraton, and headed up to Emily's room. When she opened the door, she was dressed in only her bra and panties. She held a blunt in her hand, and swung her short hair behind her shoulders. When I walked in, she handed me a blunt she'd already rolled for me.

"I roll my own shit when I don't know the person," I smiled. My phone buzzed, and I saw it was Natalia, so I just put it back up without reading it. I wanted some pussy right now, not to cuddle.

"Cool," she said, handing me what I needed. "You sure look different than you did earlier," she added.

. . .

"Yeah, so do you," I replied, licking the paper.

She turned on "Blase" by Ty Dolla $ign, and started dancing for me as I smoked. I watched as she shook her ass, making it clap and shit. Her ass was super fat, and I was enjoying the view. She danced over to me and then straddled me, putting her titties in my face. She leaned down to kiss me, and I swiftly moved out the way.

"We ain't doing all that, ma," I said as I unhooked her bra.

I took her dark, hard nipples into my mouth, and nibbled and sucked them. She dry rode me as she smoked her blunt.

"Fuck," she moaned.

She climbed off me, and then pulled my dick from my basketball shorts. She took me in her mouth, and bobbed up and down on it. She stared into my eyes as she did it, and smiled.

. . .

"Stop being cute ma, and make it sloppy," I told her.

She sat her blunt in the ashtray, and then continued slobbing me up. This was probably the weakest head I'd ever experienced. I gave up and pulled her off my dick before I went soft. She climbed on the bed, and removed her black lace thong. She spread her legs, and played with her pussy as I walked over.

"How old are you?" I asked.

"25, why?" she cocked her head to the side.

25 years old and she can't give good head. Natalia was 17 and probably gave the best head I ever had in all my 20 years. Daphne was def second in line though.

"No reason," I said.

"You wanna taste her?" she asked seductively, as she inserted three fingers into her wet pussy.

. . .

"Nah," I said as I flipped her on all fours. I slid a condom on my dick, and slid into her. Thank God the pussy was cool. Natalia had her beat in every department though.

"Damn daddy," she moaned as she started throwing it back.

Nevermind, this was not good pussy, this was a 5/10 at best. I grabbed her waist and started slamming into her walls, hoping to hurry up and cum. The sight of her fat ass bouncing, and the sound of her wet pussy were the only things keeping me hard; then all of a sudden, her shit seemed to be drying up. *Was it me?* I ain't never had this shit happen.

"Yo, you drying up. You good?" I asked. I felt my dick going limp.

"Yeah, ever since I had my son, it happens sometimes. But keep going, I will get wetter," she replied, spreading her legs some more and tooting her ass up.

"Nah, turn around," I shook my head.

. . .

She turned around and I stuck my dick in her mouth. I didn't bother removing the condom either. I grabbed the back of her head, and fucked her face for what seemed like forever. I snatched the condom off, and then shoved my dick back in her mouth just as I nutted. I had to close my eyes and picture myself sliding in and out Natalia's tight, wet walls in order to bust.

"Ahh!" she yelped as my nut dripped from her mouth. "Why you ain't say you was about to cum?" she frowned.

I shook my head and went to her bathroom to flush the condom. I used one of the towels in the bathroom to clean my dick off, then decided to just shower. When I came back out, she was chilling on her bed, scrolling on her phone.

"So I'm hoping I'll see more of you," she smirked, like she put it on me.

"Well, I live across the country ma," I replied as I got dressed.

"I live in Charleston, like Mr. Vargas, I work all his parties, so we travel together," she smiled, like that was good news.

. . .

"Oh I see, well peace," I said as I grabbed my keys and rushed out.

I got a taxi, and headed back to my room at the Four Seasons. I saw it was 1 a.m., and I couldn't believe I was out that late for a beyond lackluster fuck. I opened the text from Natalia as we rode to the room.

Baby Girl Nat: Come back Julius, we can do it.

Fuck Fuck Fuck! I just spent half the night, fucking some wack ass hoe, when I could've been fucking my own bitch. *Do better, Julius,* I told myself.

I walked into Natalia and I's hotel room, and the lights were out. Natalia was asleep, and I watched her stir as I undressed.

"Julius? Where were you?" she asked in a low tone.

"Just handling something for my boss," I lied as I climbed in bed.

. . .

"Did you see my text?" she asked. She tried to smile, and I could tell she really didn't feel good; that made me feel even worse.

"Nah, I was busy ma. I'm sorry," I replied as I kissed her lips.

She reached down into my pants to stroke my dick as we kissed passionately. I moved her hand, and put her on her back. *Damn, she was really gon' try.* That's why I loved her ass.

"Just relax ma," I replied.

I removed her panties, and ate her pussy til the damn cows came home. I didn't deserve to fuck her after sticking my dick in Mrs. Wack Walls. I made love to her pussy with my mouth until she couldn't take anymore, then we fell asleep.

For the rest of our week visit in Cali, I spent all my time with my lady. We damn near lived at the beach, and I took a gang of pictures of her in her new thong bathing suit. She was starting to show some, but she was still sexy as ever in her two-piece. Emily hit me up a couple times, but of course I ignored that bitch.

. . .

As expected, Hugo called me and let me know that he supported me moving to South Carolina, and that he didn't want to work me, which really meant he no longer needed me. I couldn't wait until he found out I had his connect, with his disloyal ass.

I tried, I really did. I tried to move on with my damn life and forget about Julius. See, y'all reading this thinking I'm just like every other jealous hoodrat you've read about in the past, but that's not the case.

I mean, you were there; Julius was my fucking man–not anyone else's, but mine. We were doing perfectly fine, and had been for a little over two years, until Natalia. I just couldn't understand what she had over me. Yes, she was beautiful, but so was I. There wasn't a day that went by where a nigga wasn't tryna holla at me. I got headaches daily, just trying to figure out what the hell went wrong.

I thought when Julius moved to South Carolina, it would be that much easier for me to get over him, and at first it was. I stayed out all night with my home girls, and even went on dates with a couple niggas who had been checking for me. I was fine, until I got home at night and was able to think. Once I was alone, Julius consumed my thoughts, and I cried myself to sleep. I wasted two years of my life with this nigga, and he completely disregarded me.

I was gon' let it go and try to live by the *"time heals all wounds"* shit, but that ended when I found out Natalia was pregnant. Although my man, bitches saw Julius as one of Indianapolis' most eligible bachelors. Anytime he made any kind of moves, it was news to the hood.

I was at work one night, and when I got into the locker room, bitches were whispering and shit. I ignored them initially as I opened my locker to get my stuff. I could see out the corner of my eye that a couple of them were staring, so I finally yelled *What!* These bitches told me that they heard through the grapevine that Ms. Natalia was pregnant.

At first I thought, *what? hell nah.* Julius didn't even get hard unless a condom was present. I brushed it off, but then it was bothering me. It was all I thought about, so I hit his ass up. He tried to ignore me, but after my many non-stop attempts...*"Yes!"* he replied to me. My heart literally sank to the pit of my stomach as I read the three letters over and over again. I wanted so badly for someone to pinch me, so I could wake up from this nightmare.

"So what you have in mind?" Greg asked as he sat in my living room.

You see, Greg didn't fuck with Julius like that no more, because when he set all his shit up in South Carolina, he excluded Greg. Greg was heated at the fact that Julius wasn't gon' put him on, so he'd do anything to help me hurt him. I thought about fucking him, but that would only hurt me more, and push Julius further away.

"I don't know. I tried showing him some pictures of her with another nigga some months back, and all he did was flip and go get her." I shook my head at the thought as I lit a cigarette.

"I'm telling you Bianca, let me go down to Charleston and seduce that nigga," Daphne smiled. I hated that he completely cut me off, but still gave her the dick here and there.

Daphne had no idea that I knew she was fucking with Julius. I thought about telling her, but as the saying goes, *keep your enemies closer.* The only reason she was here was because her little plan was my last resort. If seducing Julius would make Natalia leave, then so be it.

"So what's your plan again?" I asked for clarification.

"Simple, I'll fly down there and fuck him. I will just make sure it's recorded, and then send her the video," she smiled.

"How the fuck you gon' record it?" Greg scoffed.

"I'll set a camera up around my hotel somewhere," she nodded. "Just give me her phone number, Bianca."

This was my last resort here. If this didn't break them apart, then I was gonna throw in the fucking towel. I was tired of dedicating my life to getting Julius back.

South Carolina was beautiful. Lucy and I had only been here two weeks, but I loved it. Julius came a month before me, to get a lot of stuff straight. Lucy and I went out everyday, just to check the scenery and everything. I was eight months pregnant now, so that meant Lucy had to drive everywhere; or at least, that's what it meant to me.

I can't say that I'm not happy about having a new place to live. Julius promised that this would be a new start for us, and so far that was true. He was treating me really good, and was actually excited about the baby. He was totally different from the Julius I met late last year.

"Where are we gonna eat?" Lucy asked as we drove around town with no destination.

"You want to go to Fiery Ron's again?" For some reason, being pregnant made me crave BBQ.

"K, that's fine," Lucy replied and headed over.

After we were seated, the waitress came over to take our orders. Once she walked away, Lucy leaned in like she had a secret.

"So I have something to tell you," she started. "I'm pregnant," she added.

"You are? Why do you look so sad?" I asked, sipping my drink.

"I don't know. I guess I thought Menzo would be more serious by now."

"More serious than him asking you to move out here?" I frowned.

"That's the thing, he didn't ask me to move out here."

"Wait, what?"

"See, he told me he was moving, and I told him I wanted to come. He said it was cool if I came, but to remember that we weren't together," she dropped her head.

"But you told me he was your boyfriend."

"Wishful thinking, Nat."

I couldn't believe that Lucy would move all the way out here with no commitment. She made Victoria and I believe she and Menzo were a serious couple. I mean, Lucy has always been thirsty, but I never thought she would go this far. I shook my head as I leaned back to let the waitress sit down the food.

"So what are you gonna do about the baby?" I asked once she walked away.

"I'm gonna keep it. I guess," she shrugged.

"What did he say about the baby?"

"He wants me to keep it, but he said it doesn't change the status of our relationship," she replied, shaking her head.

After finishing our food, Lucy dropped me off at Julius and I's condo. I grabbed a cinnamon roll from the kitchen, and then headed to the stairs. I heard Julius in the other room lifting weights as I walked slowly upstairs to our bedroom. I couldn't wait to lie down in the bed and watch some TV.

While I was watching a movie on Lifetime, Julius' phone kept chiming. I tried to ignore it, but I couldn't. I looked towards the doorway to make sure he wasn't there, and grabbed the phone. I exhaled when I saw he didn't have a passcode. I clicked his messages app, which had a red #3 above it.

Franceska: I'm here in Charleston boo.

Franceska: We still on for tonight right?

Franceska: *Nevermind, I know we are. I'm gonna be at the Marriot on Lockwood Boulevard. Room 202. I love you. See you later.*

Tears fell from my eyes onto his phone as I read the messages over and over again. I was so into what I was reading that I didn't hear Julius walk in.

"Natalia, hey baby girl," he said.

I looked up from his phone, and towards the door at him. He stormed over to me and snatched his phone out of my hand. I flinched a little, hoping he wouldn't hit me.

"Who is Franceska?" I asked through tears.

"Why the fuck you going through my shit, Natalia?" he asked as he stared down at me, with an angry expression.

"I-it was ringing and I-"

"Don't you ever go looking through my phone again," he said as he walked towards the bathroom.

"Julius who is she?" I asked with tears running down my face. "She said she loved you," I cried.

"She ain't no fucking body! She just another one of them hoes that stay in my phone," he replied.

"You love her too?" I asked.

"Hell nah! I can't believe you'd even ask me that shit. Only girl I love is the one living in this condo with me," he smiled. I stared at him, not knowing what to think. He walked over to me, and kissed my lips. "You my girl, nobody else," he said as he looked down into my eyes. I nodded, then turned to walk away. He came up behind me and hugged me. He rubbed my belly, and placed kisses on my neck. "I love you," he said.

"I love you too."

Later that night, while relaxing in bed, I watched as Julius got dressed to go handle some *business.* I knew he was going to see Franceska, and it broke my heart. I wanted to follow him, but I was too tired right now to be doing all that. My phone buzzed, and Frank's name flashed across. I had been talking to him a couple times a week ever since I moved.

Frank: *Missin' you ma.*

As I was about to reply, Julius walked over to me and kissed my lips.

"I'll be back around 10 p.m. Let me know if need any food or anything, okay?" he said, and I nodded. "Natalia, that girl was nobody aight?" he said as he lifted my chin.

I half smiled, and he hopped up to leave.

Me: *Frank you can't text me things like that. Lol*

Frank: *Man, fuck that nigga. He don't even treat you right, why you still with him?*

Me: *Love.*

Frank: *So how you feel about me?*

Me: *I think you're sweet and cool.*

Frank was a really nice guy, and really sexy, but I was in love with Julius. There was no way I could leave Julius for Frank. Plus, Julius would kill us both.

Frank: *That's for now. Watch.*

Me: *Lol, whatever.*

Frank: *Wyd? Let's FaceTime.*

My dreams were actually a reality right now. Bart proved to be legit as fuck, and I had a full on operation running. It was obviously still in its beginning stages, but the money coming in was way more than that chump change Hugo was shooting down to me.

The team I recruited a couple months back was still down for the cause when I moved out here, and that put me at ease. We were moving so much weight that I had to up my shipment amount with Bart. That nigga loved money, so he was more than happy. I was a little worried that if I asked for a bigger shipment, he may not have been able to fulfill it, but my nigga came through.

My brother Rashad and my boys Tim, Dash, and Leese were living well too. These niggas were used to living in beat up ass apartments back in Indianapolis. Now, they had nice condos like me, and a damn car. They never had cars when we lived in Indiana. I laughed at my thoughts. All this was done off only a month of damn work. I couldn't wait to see how much we were gonna have as time progressed.

Bart also told me that Hugo was having a hard time with his operation now that I wasn't working for him no more. I felt kind of bad, but then I thought about how he was so willing to let me go for a connect. Yeah, Bart was a phenomenal connect, but Hugo knew he couldn't move as much work without me; a catch 22 for him, I guess. All I knew was that I was a muthafucking Kingpin on the rise, and I was loving that shit.

I pulled up to the Marriot on Lockwood, and parked my whip. I double-checked my texts to see what room number Franceska said she was in. I couldn't believe Natalia had seen her messages. Lowkey, my heart was beating fast, hoping she didn't try to bounce on me.

Regardless of me smashing hoes on the side, I loved Natalia's sexy ass. Everything about her was A-1, but it was hard to deny all the pussy being thrown my way. Bitches was willing to be my side piece and everything, even when I was broke, so I could only imagine how it's gon' be when I start stacking them millions.

"Hey papi," Franceska smiled.

"What's up?" I said, walking into her room.

I plopped down on the bed and exhaled. I was tired as hell from being out all damn day, checking my traps and building relationships with the crooked law enforcement. Only reason I came to see Franceska was because I promised her I would see her if she visited. I couldn't believe she flew all the way out here just to see me. I didn't know if it was thirst, or if she really just liked me.

"I been missing you, Ju," she said, walking over and sitting next to me.

"Word?" I asked, lighting up the blunt she handed me.

"Hell yeah. Ever since you got you a little girlfriend, you been dissing me, papi."

"I ain't been dissing you, ma; I been busy. I'm running things now, which means I got way more responsibility," I said, taking a pull off the blunt.

"Yeah, I get it. So what's up, you gon' let me be on the side?" she asked.

"That's what you want?"

"Well, I'd much rather be your main bitch, but I know you love your little Natalia," she replied, blowing smoke out.

"Glad you already know. I ain't got time for a side bitch though," I replied honestly. I only had time for my baby girl, and a few meaningless fuck sessions on the side.

"Well let me show you what you can get by fucking with me then," she said, putting her blunt out.

She removed her dress, and she was ass naked under it. She had my name tatted right between her perky breasts. Wow. I leaned back, propping myself up with my elbows as she removed my dick from my pants. She took all eleven inches in, and sloppily sucked the life out of me. I cupped the back of her head, and gently fucked her face. She sped up her motions, and I nutted down her throat. I stood up, removed my clothes, and then pushed her onto the bed on all fours.

"I want you to taste me papi," she purred. *Um, nah.*

"You know that ain't on the menu of options," I replied, opening a condom.

"Let's try it without one tonight," she said, looking over her shoulder.

I ignored her and once the condom was on, I slid inside her wet walls. I grabbed her hair, and thrusted into her roughly. I smacked her fat ass, and watched it jiggle as I pumped.

"Fuck you got some good dick, Ju!" she moaned. I felt her gush all over my pole, which made me harder.

"Fuck," I said in a low tone, as I moved in and out of her slowly.

"I'm about to cum again, baby. Ah, oh my gosh!" she moaned in a high-pitched voice as she came again.

Her body jerked a little as I sped up, tearing her shit up. Once I felt my nut rising, I pulled out, took off the condom, and then turned her around to nut in her mouth. She swallowed it, and then cleaned some off the head of my dick.

"Shit," I said as I watched her.

I walked to her bathroom to flush the condom, and clean my dick off. I came back into the room, and immediately started getting dressed.

"You can't spend the night?" Franceska pouted.

"Nah, ma," I replied. I was not gon' spend the night. Only bitch I was laying next to was Natalia.

"Okay, can we see each other tomorrow?"

"Prolly not, I got a lot of business to handle," I replied, looking for my phone. I spotted it, and saw I had messages from Rashad, Tim, Dash, Daphne, and Emily's wack ass. I was surprised Natalia hadn't text me.

"Well I can wait up as late as you wan-"

I cut her off by putting my finger in the air while I called Natalia.

"Hello?"

"You hungry, baby girl? You need anything?" I asked.

"Since it's only 9:05 can you go to Chick-Fil-A?" she asked.

"Of course baby. Text what you want, okay?"

"Okay."

"I love you, Nat," I said, hoping she said it back.

"I love you too Julius," she replied, and I could hear her smiling.

I disconnected the call, and saw Franceska rolling her eyes. I thought my eyes were deceiving me, but there was an actual tear rolling down her face. I didn't have time for this shit, and I needed to get my baby's food before they closed.

"Aight, see you later ma," I told Franceska, and headed out.

"You not even gon' ask me why I'm crying?" she said sniffling.

"Why you crying?" I asked after sighing.

"Fuck it Ju, since you act like it's a fucking chore to care about my feelings," she spat.

"Fasho, peace," I said, and left.

Not even five minutes later, my phone was ringing and it was Franceska. I didn't answer because I needed to focus on getting my girl's food before they closed. Once I ordered, I saw she was calling again. She hadn't stopped calling the whole way to Chick-Fil-A.

"What? Damn, why you blowing me up?" I frowned as I waited to get to the food pick-up window.

"I'm sorry, Ju. But hearing you tell her you love her made me feel some type of way," she whined.

"You do realize that Natalia is my girl, right?" I frowned as if she could see me.

"Yeah I know, that's why I wanted to call and apologize," she replied somberly.

"Oh aight then."

"Well, just know that I do love you, regardless if you love me or not," she added.

"Goodnight Franceska," I replied, and disconnected the call.

These meaningless fuck sessions I had on the side were proving to be a damn handful. These chicks were acting as if they found a piece of gold, or a rare diamond. They just needed to understand that Natalia and I were in it for the long haul–no ifs, ands, or buts about it.

NATALIA

2 WEEKS LATER

Since I was about to pop any minute, Julius didn't want me cleaning and stuff around the house so today, Lucy was going to help me interview some girls.

Nothing really fit at this moment, so I threw on a blue maxi dress that stopped a little bit above my knees. I slid into my fuzzy house slippers, and put my long hair into a low bun, with a part down on the side.

"What time is the first one coming?" Lucy asked.

"At 2 p.m.," I said as I grabbed a notepad.

I looked at the time, and saw it was around 1:50 p.m. After we got everything together, including having snacks for any waiting intervie-wees, we sat and waited.

"Hello, I'm Natalia and this is my best friend Lucy," I smiled at the 4:00 appointment. I was exhausted from all the interviews by this time.

"Hello Natalia, and Lucy," she replied, shaking our hands.

"So what do you know about being a maid? Have you ever been one?" Lucy asked.

"Oh yes! I'm from the Dominican Republic, and that is how my mother made money to support us. By the time I was 16, I was assisting her with the houses she worked," the girl smiled.

"How old are you now?" I asked.

"I'm 23," she smiled. "I can do a trial run, and if you don't like it, I will leave without pay," she added.

"Can't beat that shit," Lucy chuckled, and so did I.

"Well when can you start?" I asked.

"How is tomorrow morning?" she smiled.

"That's good, because my boyfriend will be here to meet you," I smiled.

Right," she half smiled.

We all stood up simultaneously, and shook hands. We talked a little bit more before I showed her out.

"Did you notice how she seemed to be bothered by the mention of your boyfriend?" Lucy raised a brow.

"Yeah, I wonder why?"

"Maybe she is a lesbian, and was hoping she could be with you," Lucy smiled.

"I doubt it, look at my obvious pregnant belly," I chuckled.

"Hey, maybe that bitch is a freak!"

We laughed in unison, and then continued to relax with each other all day.

———

I was laying down sleep in the bed when I heard a bunch of rustling. I knew it was Julius, and butterflies filled my stomach. Still til this day, he made me feel so nervous. I pressed the home button on my phone to see the time, and it was 2 a.m. I climbed out of the bed, wearing sweat shorts and a bra only. Right as I was walking to the door, he came in.

"What you doing up baby girl?" he asked.

"I heard you come in," I smiled.

He walked closer to me, and kissed my lips. He started to undress down to his boxers, and let out a sigh.

"Are you okay?" I asked.

"Yeah baby, how are you feeling?" he asked.

"I'm uncomfortable, I couldn't sleep," I replied as I walked over to him.

"You wanna take a bath with me?" he asked, and I nodded.

We headed over to the bathroom, and he ran us some nice, hot bathwater. We submerged ourselves in the water, and it soothed my muscles. I sat between his legs as he massaged my back. He planted kisses on the nape of my neck and my shoulder.

"I hired a maid today," I said.

"Oh yeah? That was fast."

"Yeah she was nice, and she's been doing it a long time. Is it okay that I hired one already?"

"Of course babe," he replied.

I leaned back against him, and he rubbed down my belly. His hands reached my kitten, and he started to play with my clit. He dipped his finger inside me, and started to thrust in and out.

"Ohhh ahh. Julius," I moaned.

He brought his free arm around to turn my face back for a kiss. He tongued me down, while plunging his fingers in between my legs. He sped up, and bit his lip as he stared into my eyes.

"Ahh ah," I whimpered before exploding on his finger.

He removed it, then licked my juices off. We washed each other off, and then laid down in the bed. The only position we could really do was spooning, so he got behind me and lifted my leg up. He slid into me, and started slowly pumping.

"Damn, baby girl. Fuck," he moaned as he craned his neck around to kiss my lips.

He kept his thrusts nice and slow, and it was driving me crazy. He moved his hips in a circular motion, while hitting my spot that only he could find. He sucked my bottom lip, then the top one. I closed my eyes to enjoy the feeling, until he told me to look at him. He always wanted to keep eye contact with me while we fucked. *I want you to be looking me in the eyes when you cum*, he'd always say.

"I'm cumming Julius!" I whined as I felt my pelvis tighten.

My body jerked as I released onto his long, thick pole. He gripped my leg tighter, still holding it up in the air. He kept moving slowly in and out of me in a circular motion. He was going in fast, and then sliding out slow. He did that constantly, and I felt another orgasm rising.

"I want you to cum again for me, baby," he said, looking me in the eyes as I looked at him over my shoulder. "Give daddy what he wants," he said as he kissed my lips soft and slow. He was driving me crazy. No wonder he had me so gone.

"Daddy, I'm cumming again," I moaned softly.

"Me too, make your dick cum," he said, not losing eye contact with me, and placing soft kisses on my lips here and there.

I lifted my leg a little more, giving him even more access. He grabbed my ass, and spread my cheeks. He stared down as he pumped into me a little faster than before, but still nice and slow. I loved how he could switch it up. He could fuck me rough, or he could go slow, and I would still cum hard.

"Tell me what you want," he said.

"I want you to cum, daddy. Cum in your pussy," I moaned.

"Say no more," he smiled, and then kissed my lips.

He kept his lips pressed to mine as he sped up a little, then we came together. He pumped me super slow, making sure all his seeds were being released, while tonguing me down.

"Fuck Julius," I chuckled, and so did he.

"Yo pussy is off the fucking wall ma," he said as he laid on his back and stared at the ceiling. "I never wanted that shit to end," he chuckled.

"I love you," I said as I nuzzled up to him, and laid on his chest.

"I love you more, Nat," he replied as he panted out of breath. "And that award winning ass pussy," he laughed, and so did I.

After that little session of lovemaking, I was able to fall right asleep in my baby's arms. I loved him so much, and nothing or no one would ever change that.

JULIUS

Today was gon' be a long fucking day. I had a couple meetings set up, plus a phone call from Hugo. Yes, I made that nigga schedule a time to call me. I'm a busy man, and I no longer work for him

I admit, I was feeling myself a little bit because the money was pouring in something crazy. Bart was right about the streets out here being dry, even though that was something I already knew. These muthafuckas were so hungry out here that they'd take anything, and on top of that, I actually had good shit.

People were already kissing my ass, and I hadn't even been here that long. The perks were flying in left and right; free club invites and I'm only 20, automatic VIP when I'm there, and all kinds of shit. As I assumed, the women were much more aggressive than back home in Indiana, cause a nigga's pockets had gotten fatter. Did I enjoy it? Not really, because they were thirsty as fuck, and always did way too much just for some dick. Now my brother Rashad on the other hand, and Tim, were indulging in every bit of pussy getting thrown their damn way.

I walked into the bathroom to brush my teeth and take my shower.

Once I rinsed my mouth with mouthwash, I walked into the hallway to get some towels.

"Mr. Tate."

I knew I recognized the voice, but this person definitely shouldn't be in my fucking house. I turned around to confirm what I already knew.

"Franceska? What the fuck you doing here?" I frowned.

"I work here, Mr. Tate. Your wife knows me as simply Lisa," she smiled and winked.

Natalia walked up the stairs of the condo, and I was hoping she didn't hear what we were talking about.

"Babe, uh who is this?" I smiled.

"Lisa, the maid I hired," she replied, and Franceska looked at her and smiled. "What's wrong?" she asked.

Franceska was smiling from ear to fucking ear, and it was pissing me off. I'll be damned if this bitch was gon' be up in my shit, cleaning and trying to be sneaky. I had something for this bitch though.

I walked up to Natalia and towered over her. I dipped my tongue in her mouth, and began to kiss her passionately as fuck. She tried to back up some, but I rushed her into the wall. She finally gave in, and I continued to tongue her down.

"I love you," I said.

"I love you too," she replied out of breath.

I turned around to see Franceska, and she was glaring at me. Her eyes were glazed over, and I knew that in any minute, she'd be crying. Regardless of her just being hired, I was gon' fire her ass.

After my meeting with my peoples, I dismissed everybody and waited for Hugo's call. I knew he'd be calling in a couple minutes, so I decided to check a couple notifications. On time, my iPhone rang, and I placed it on speakerphone.

"What's up Hugo?" I said non-chalantly.

"Julius Tate, thanks for penciling me in," he said sarcastically.

"What did you need to talk to me about?" I asked, getting straight to the point.

"I mean, I don't know where to start. I put you on to this shit, and how do you repay me? By stealing my fucking connect, and running off to Charleston?" he boomed through my phone.

"Hold up my nigga–yes you put me on, and I thank you for that. However, don't try to make it seem like you have anything to do with the success that I have out here in South Carolina, homie."

"I don't?" he asked surprised.

"Hell fucking nah you don't! I built this shit from scratch. For almost a year, I busted my ass, flying back and forth, proving myself, and building relationships out here so that I could have my own shit! All the while still pushing weight for you!" I yelled, feeling myself get angrier.

"Yeah, thanks to my fucking connect!"

"Your connect chose me, nigga! I went to Los Angeles to get him for *yo* ungrateful ass! Even after he damn near begged to go into business with me, I still was trying to get him for you instead!"

"And how long did that fucking last! You ain't loyal to shit! I send you to California to help me out, and you not only move to South Carolina, but take the damn connect with you!" he yelled.

"I'm not loyal? I'm not fucking loyal? The only reason I accepted his offer was because when he told you to get rid of me, you agreed without protesting even once, Hugo! You didn't do so much as inquire as to why he felt the way he did about me! And I tested you to see if you would really let me go, and you did!"

He paused for a while, because I guess he didn't know that I knew.

"Like I said, you only where you at cause of me. You wouldn't even have Bart as a connect if I hadn't sent you!"

"Is that what you think? I bet you had no idea that he requested me to meet him because he had no intention of working with yo ass. He was intending to be my connect the whole time."

"And all that shit you talking about not stepping on toes," he scoffed.

"Hugo, be grateful that I didn't just take over your shit, because you know I could've," I replied calmly. I was done with this conversation.

"You just watch your back, nigga," he replied, ignoring my previous statement because he knew I was right.

"You know your threats mean nothing to me Hugo, so save it. I'll be sleeping peacefully, with both eyes closed tonight like always. Have a good one, and let me know if you need to borrow some money, I heard ya pockets is drying up," I laughed, and disconnected the call.

Hugo had me fucked up and like I said before, if he wanted to go to war, I could do that. If he tried to fuck with me, I would take over Indianapolis and have him in an alley begging for change.

Hugo was smart, but I was smarter. This nigga didn't invest his money into shit. He made millions, and blew it on nice houses, cars, and whatever other material possessions he could get his hands on. Never did he invest in any businesses, or put his money up to save. While being here in Charleston, I'd already invested in a couple stocks and two Regal Cinemas movie theatres, and I wasn't done yet. I was not playing around, especially with a son on the way.

While working for Hugo, I saved a lot of my shit. I shopped here and there, but I never got shit I didn't need. I got me one nice ass whip, my Lexus, and a cool little crib. Everything else, I put up. I was rich enough to not work for about three years, but I wanted to be wealthy; wealthy enough to where if I did decide to leave the game, I would never have to worry. I wanted that money that couldn't even be spent in one lifetime. It looked like I was gon' make it happen too, with the way money was coming in. I had discipline when it came to money; maybe not with women, but when it came to money, I could do the damn thing. As far as the women, I never thought about working on that, but now that I had Natalia, I was gonna see what I could do.

As I headed out of my office, which was still slightly under construction, my phone buzzed in my pocket letting me know I had a text.

Daphne: Hey boo.

Me: Sup.

Daphne: *Guess who's in Charleston?*

Why the fuck were these bitches following me?

Me: *I hope not you.*

Daphne: *Too bad lol. I wanna see you tonight.*

Me: *That might be possible.*

Daphne: *Can you come to my hotel tonight?*

Me: *Maybe around 11pm if I'm done with business.*

Work always came before the hoes.

Daphne: *Cool. See you later daddy.*

I went to the gym to shoot some hoops with my brother Rashad, and my boy Dash. I hadn't done that in awhile, and that said a lot for a nigga who was used to working out a couple times a week. Lately I had been too busy, and too damn tired to do anything.

"I swear I've never seen an ass that was as fat as hers," Dash laughed, showing us how fat with his hands.

"You talking about old girl from that club the other night?" I asked. I remembered smashing her home girl, whose ass was just as fat.

"Hell yeah nigga. Pussy was fire too, I may have to double back," he replied.

"What's up with Natalia's homegirl Paula?" Rashad asked.

Paula was this chick that Natalia met while out here. She took a liking to her, because she had a daughter and they bonded over being mothers or some shit. That's what Natalia said. She, Lucy, and newly Paula were thick as thieves these days.

"Nigga I don't know. But aye, I'm about to get up outta here, we been here for five hours," I chuckled, standing up.

"Aight man, but tell Natalia to holla at Paula for me," Rashad added.

"Fasho."

I dapped both of them up, then headed home to shower. After showering, I let Natalia know I was headed to take care of some business, and then headed to Daphne's hotel. She was staying at the same one that I met Franceska at awhile back. Speaking of her, I been too busy to even fire her ass, but I would ASAP.

Me: *Room?*

Daphne: *210*

I locked my phone up, and then headed inside. I spotted Franceska in the lobby, and tried to keep walking. Unfortunately, she spotted me, and called after me.

"What Franceska? I'm busy," I replied, walking to the elevator.

"Where you going, Ju? You here to meet another bitch?" she asked with an attitude.

"Whoa, you ain't in a position to question me," I spat.

Once I got to the second floor, I walked to Daphne's room, with Franceska hot on my heels.

I heard a knock at my room door, so I made sure the cameras were on and recording. Bianca thought I was doing this for her but no, I wanted Julius for my damn self. *Fuck Bianca!*

I made sure the camera was well hidden, then walked to the door. I peeked through the peephole, and saw Julius along with some Spanish bitch. I swung open the door to see what was up.

"Julius, who is this babe?" I asked, cocking my head to the side.

"Babe? I'm something like his woman. Franceska," she replied.

Julius simply scoffed, and walked into the room past me.

"You're sexy, why don't you stay?" I told the Franceska chick.

She paused, and then smiled as if she had an idea. I knew she was not gonna leave and let me and Julius fuck, so she might as well join in.

We started smoking a couple blunts, and drinking Grey Goose straight. We were getting fucked up and listening to music. "Fuck a Bitch" by the Game was playing as we smoked our last blunt. Franceska started to undress, as Julius stared at her lustfully. She danced for him, and he was definitely giving her all his attention. While he was looking at her, I made sure the red recording light on my hidden camera was still on. I looked back over, and Franceska was in her white lace underwear set, kissing down Julius' chiseled upper body. She removed his dick, and started to go to work on it. I got behind her, and pulled her thong down. She stepped out of it, while slobbing on Julius. I plunged two fingers into her opening from the back, and reached my other hand around to play with her clit. My pussy got wetter at the thought of little innocent Natalia seeing this tape.

"Ahhh fuck, shit," Franceska cried out. "Give me that nut daddy," she said to Julius, as she continued to suck him up.

"Here it comes, fuck," Julius groaned, as he palmed the back of her head. "Ahh shit," he moaned as he threw his head back, nutting in her mouth. She simultaneously came on my fingers, and I licked it up.

Julius tried to sit up, but I pushed his sexy ass back on the bed and took his dick into my mouth.

"Aww damn," he moaned as I bobbed up and down on his dick. Julius loved my head game.

As I worked my gag free magic on him, Franceska lifted my teddy and began sucking my clit from the back. She fingered me at the same time, and that shit was taking me over the edge.

"Ahhh, I'm cumming. Fuck!" I whimpered.

I dipped down and sucked on Julius' balls for a little bit, then trailed from his balls back to his dick. I felt his dick get harder, and I knew he was about to cum. I sped up while playing with his balls, and he nutted all down my throat. I came in Franceska's mouth, and she licked me clean. I threw her on her back and dipped my head between her legs to taste her. I watched as Julius put a condom on, with his *always-gotta-have-safe-sex ass*, and then held my breath as he thrusted into me. As he fucked the shit out of me, I brought Franceska to ecstasy, sucking on her swollen clit. Once she came, she told Julius to come here by waving her index finger. He pulled out of me as my nut dripped down my thighs. He always made me bust hard.

Julius laid down on the bed, and Franceska mounted his monster. I thought about sitting on his face, but I knew he might bust my ass over the head. Unbeknownst to him, I knew only Natalia got that treatment. He tried to make it seem like he just didn't do it, but Bianca been put me on game. I couldn't wait to claim him as mine, and feel his soft lips on my pussy. As Franceska rode his dick like a damn professional jockey, I sucked on his balls.

"Oh my fucking gosh yo!" he yelled out.

"Daddy, I'm about to cum. Ahhh," Franceska moaned as Julius played with her nipples.

I played with my clit, as I sucked on his balls, and soon enough we all came together. Julius laid down for a bit, then went to the bathroom to clean himself. I rolled some more blunts, and when he came back I handed him and Franceska one. We smoked and drank some more, and fucked all night. For the first time, Julius slept over.

In the middle of the night, I turned off the camera and slipped it back in my bag. I went back to bed to lay down with my soon to be man, with Franceska on the other side of him.

Julius didn't come home last night, and I cried myself to sleep for the fourth time this week. I knew it wasn't good for the baby, but I was so miserable. When he came home this morning, he showered and left right back out. This wasn't supposed to be like this. When we moved, I assumed he would be different, and for the first couple weeks he was.

My phone buzzed, and I wiped my tears to see better. I was hoping it was Julius, but when I looked, I saw it was Frank.

Frank: *Good morning, how are you?*

Me: *I'm okay.*

Frank and I had been texting non-stop. I knew it wasn't good for me to be in contact with him like this, but I was lonely.

Frank: *Just okay? What that nigga do?*

Me: *Didn't come home for the fourth night in a row.*

I knew I shouldn't be discussing my relationship with another man, but I knew Lucy was tired of my complaining.

Frank: *You should come visit.*

Me: *You know I can't do that.*

Frank text me back, but I saw I received a message from another number. I backed out of our conversation, and clicked the unknown number. I saw it was a video, and I was scared to click it cause it may have been some kind of virus. Curiosity got the best of me, and I clicked it. I watched for a couple seconds, until I realized what it was. It was Julius having sex with the chick I caught sucking his dick in his car that day, and our fucking maid.

I had never been so mad in my life. Here I was crying myself to sleep, and he was out fucking all kinds of hoes. I'm pregnant with his fucking baby, and this is what he does?

Me: *Fuck you Julius. I'm so done.*

I attached the video for him to watch, and text Frank.

Me: *Do you think you could get me a ticket to Indianapolis right now? I will pay you back I swear.*

Frank: *Hell yeah ma, I will text once it's done.*

Me: *Thank you so much!*

Frank: *No, thank you.*

I hopped up, and pulled out my trusty duffle bag. I threw a whole bunch of clothes in it, and made sure to pack some of the baby stuff that I'd gotten while out here. I knew Julius wouldn't respond for at least an hour, because that's just the type of nigga he was. He didn't give a fuck about me, and I didn't know how many times I needed him to show me that. I was done packing in about 30 minutes and checked my phone. I saw a text from Frank telling me it was done, and a screenshot of my flight details. I dialed Lucy, because I needed a ride.

"Lucy, please take me to the airport," I said as soon as she answered.

"Why, what's up?" she asked.

"It's an emergency," I lied. I knew she would protest if I told her why. I would tell her once I touched down.

"Damn, what happened?"

"Look, can you just hurry?' I asked.

"Aight, on my way. Damn."

I hung up before she could even finish, and then ran down stairs. I still had no calls or texts from Julius, so I still had time. Lucy arrived in about ten minutes, and we sped off towards the airport since my flight was in only two hours.

"Thank you babe. And please don't tell anyone where I'm going, okay?" I said with the passenger door open.

"Why Natalia? What's going on?"

"Just promise me."

"Aight I promise," she said, smacking her lips.

"I will let you know what's going on once I arrive to Indiana," I smiled, and closed the door.

After getting to my gate, I relaxed for about an hour until it was boarding time. I smiled at the fact that Frank had gotten me a first class ticket. Maybe I should give him a chance; he seemed to really care about me. I shrugged at my thoughts, as my phone buzzed.

Boyfriend: *Natalia, ma. Answer your phone baby girl.*

Boyfriend: *Nvm, I'll be home in 20 minutes. Don't do nothing crazy, I can explain!*

I shook my head, and walked onto the plane. He was gon' get a nice surprise when he came home looking for me. I turned my iPhone on airplane mode, and then prepared for my flight to Indiana.

JULIUS

Natalia hit me up about some bullshit a couple hours ago. I was fuming after seeing that fucking video of Daphne, Franceska, and I. I wanted to beat Daphne's ass, because I knew she was behind this shit.

I checked my phone as I drove home, to see if Natalia replied to my text. She hadn't, so I just put my phone away. I would just talk to her when I got home later tonight. I told her 20 minutes, but I had to check up on a couple things first.

One of my workers said someone tried to come through and rob them. They said the nigga told them that he knew me. I was confused as hell, because I knew my niggas like the back of my hand, and I knew they wouldn't do me like that. Also, I was paying them quite handsomely, so there was no need for them to rob a fucking trap.

I pulled up to the trap, and threw my shit in park. No addicts were hanging around, and that was a good look. I didn't need any attention drawn to my shit. I walked in and saw my niggas Terry and Alonzo inside. They were the ones who told me about the incident. They were able to tussle with the nigga and get his gun, but of course he got away.

"What's up Julius?" Alonzo and Terry said as they dapped me up.

"Sup, so what the fuck happened?" I frowned.

"Nigga showed up here trying to get something for free. He said he knew you, and when we denied his request, he pulled out a gun. He started waving it around, saying we needed to give him any money that was in here, and all this other shit," Terry started.

"Did he say his name? Or was anybody with him that said his name?" I asked.

"Nah boss," Alonzo replied.

"What he look like?"

"Short, light-skinned, with braids," Alonzo answered, and Terry nodded.

"Aight, thanks," I said and bounced.

The description they gave me sounded just like Greg. However, Greg lived in Indianapolis; I was so confused right now. I pulled away from the curb to head home to my baby girl. I decided to shoot Greg a text and see what was up.

Me: Where you at?

Greg: Home, chilling.

Me: Aight, I'm finna come through. I'm in town.

I wanted to see if he would protest. If he did, I knew he was here in Charleston. If he didn't, I was back to square one on who tried to rob my shit. Damn, I wasn't even here that long and niggas was already acting crazy.

Greg: When I said home, I meant my new girl's crib. I'm tryna fuck her right now, so I ain't into having no company. Lol

Bingo.

Me: Oh aight. Peace.

I was gon' take care of Greg, but for now I needed to go talk to my lady. I sped home and hopped out quick.

"Natalia," I called out as I walked up the stairs.

I didn't get a response. I called her name again, as I walked into the bedroom we shared. I looked around, and immediately spotted her empty closet. *No. No. She didn't leave, did she?* I pulled out my phone and dialed her immediately. She didn't pick up, so I hung up and called her ass again.

"What!" she finally picked up.

"Yo where you at?" I asked.

"I'm gone."

"Obviously ma, but to where? Lucy and Menzo's?"

"I'm not in South Carolina, Julius."

"What? What you mean you not in fucking South Carolina, Natalia?!" I yelled.

"I don't want to be with you anymore, Julius. You hurt me too much," she started to cry.

"Baby, give me a chance to explain. Where you at?"

"Don't worry about it. I will let you know when the baby is here," she replied sniffling.

"Natalia! Don't fuck with me! I ain't the one! Where the fuck are you?!" I was so fucking mad, I felt my veins protruding from my neck. "Are you in Indiana?" I asked.

"No."

Click.

I pulled the phone away from my ear, and saw she hung up. I called her back five times, and she sent me to voicemail each time.

Me: *Natalia, please baby.*

Today was not my fucking day, but it wasn't gon' be Daphne's either. I pulled out my phone, and shot her a text.

Me: *Aye this bitch Natalia tripping, wyd?*

Daphne: *Chilling, smoking.*

Me: *Aight, I'm gon' come get you.*

Daphne: *Can't wait.*

I hopped in my whip, and sped to the Marriott on Lockwood. Once I arrived, I sent her ass a text to let her know that I was here. I double-checked for my gun, to make sure it was there. Yes, I had a gun. Overboard? Hell fucking nah. I loved Natalia more than any fucking thing, and anybody that got in the way of that had to go, simple.

"Damn, took you forever to call. I'm going back to Indiana the day after tomorrow," she smiled as she got in.

"My bad ma, I been busy," I said, putting the car in drive.

"So Natalia tripping on you?" she asked.

"Yeah, same shit," I said pulling up to an abandoned warehouse/farm I'd just obtained. "Why the fuck you set me up?" I asked Daphne, as I held my Glock to her head.

"Okay wait, ain't nobody set you up, Ju!" she said with her hands up.

"You sent a video of us fucking to Natalia's phone, bitch!"

She opened and closed her mouth as her mind raced, looking for a lie to tell me. I reached over her, and pushed her out my passenger side.

"Wait Julius, please! Bian-" she begged as she sat in the dirt.

I pulled the trigger and emptied two bullets between her eyes. I called Leese and Dash to get the clean up crew, then bounced. When I got home, I called Natalia a couple more times and got no answer.

"Fuck!" I yelled, throwing my phone against the wall.

I don't know why I hadn't moved back to Indiana earlier. I guess I was being stupid, and I was in love. I still am in love, but I just can't continue to let Julius treat me such a way.

"How's that feel?" Frank asked as he massaged my feet.

He'd been so good to me as usual. I was really starting to feel bad for not giving him a chance prior. I still didn't know if I should, because I was still hung up on stupid Julius.

"Feels too good," I replied, throwing my head back.

"You want to go to dinner tonight?" he asked.

"Hmmm, we've been going every night since I've been here," I smiled.

"So, you haven't been enjoying it?" he chuckled.

"No, I definitely have. I just don't want you spending all your money."

"I don't mind spending money on my lady," he smirked.

His lady? I never agreed to us being in a relationship. I mean, look at me. I'm at full term with another man's child.

"Frank I-"

"Natalia, don't do this to me, ma. What have I been doing wrong, babe?" he asked, with pleading eyes.

"Nothing I just-"

"Just give me a chance, Natalia. I'm so in love with you, I can't take all this shit. One day you in my face, the next you back with him."

"Okay," I replied, knowing I didn't want to be with him. I didn't want anybody right in this moment. My heart was broken.

"Yes!" he smiled big as hell, and then got up to kiss me. "I'm gon' treat you how that nigga should treat you," he nodded.

We decided to go to Delicia's since I had a taste for Mexican food. I was starved and couldn't wait to get some food in my mouth. I looked over the menu while we waited to be seated, so I already knew what I wanted when the waitress came over.

"Hungry?" Frank laughed, because I ordered a lot.

"Yes, remember I'm eating for two people," I smiled.

"What are you naming the baby?" he asked as he sipped his water.

I was about to answer, but my phone buzzed. I took it out, and saw that it was Julius yet again. He'd been calling and texting me everyday, trying to find out where I was. I knew I needed to tell him so that he wouldn't miss the birth of our son.

Boyfriend: Natalia, I'm not gon' stop asking where you are. I will turn every state out looking for you. Don't make me do that.

Me: Indiana, I'm staying in a hotel. I will let you know which one, whenever I go into labor. Just be available.

Boyfriend: How soon?

Me: It'll be sometime this week.

Boyfriend: Okay, I love you Natalia Thomas.

"Can you not text your ex when we literally just made it official a couple hours ago?" Frank frowned.

"He's the father of my baby, Frank; I have to talk to him sometime."

"Not really," he replied.

"What? Yes I do-"

"I'm done talking about him. Now I asked what you were naming the baby," he spat, staring me in the eyes.

***

"What are you doing babe?" Frank asked, peeking into my room.

"I-I was thinking I should go to a hotel," I stuttered.

"Why? Is it about our conversation earlier? I'm sorry, Nat. I was just a little jealous," he smiled as he walked over to me. "You forgive me?" he asked hugging me, and I nodded. "Aight, we can share a room now that this is official," he smiled and grabbed my hand to lead me to his room.

He pulled the covers back for me to lay down, and then climbed in next to me. I laid on my back staring at the ceiling, until I felt his hand go between my legs.

"Frank no."

"Why? What's the fucking problem, Natalia? You said we together!" he scowled.

"Just not with the baby in here. After I have the baby," I said, hoping he would go for it.

"Fine. But after the baby, this has got to happen," he said before turning his back to me.

My phone buzzed on the nightstand, and I quickly grabbed it, not wanting to wake up Frank. I saw it was Julius, and a tear escaped my eye. I missed him so much, and Frank was making me uncomfortable.

Boyfriend: *I'm here, do I still have to wait until you go into labor to see you?*

"Natalia! Go to sleep! It's 2 a.m.!" Frank yelled, making me jump.

I locked my phone, and placed it under my pillow. I heard Julius text me about 30 minutes later, and I cried when I couldn't answer. I drifted off to sleep a couple hours later.

JULIUS

Natalia was pissing me off. I didn't like the fact that she was out here with my baby, and refusing to tell where she was. I was calling and texting her constantly since I'd been here, and she would only reply sometimes.

Tonight, I decided to go out and relax to take my mind off her. This shit was stressing me the fuck out.

I headed to Black Light to see some strippers, since clubs wouldn't let me in at my age. It was only in South Carolina where my name meant something. Hopefully that shit would change though. If Hugo fucked with me, I would come take over his shit. I already knew the turf, so it wouldn't be hard at all.

I walked into the club, and some song I didn't recognize was blasting. It was a lot of new bitches here that I'd never seen before when I lived in Indiana. I saw a couple associates I knew, so I went ahead and sat with them.

"Wow, long time no see player!" my homie Gerald smiled.

"I know, had to make that move," I smiled.

"How's that working out for you?"

"Business wise, great, personal life is hella rocky though," I shook my head.

"Ain't it always like that. And then when your personal life gets in order, the money dry up!" he joked, and we laughed.

We watched a couple strippers do their thing, and got a couple lap dances as well. I saw it was 1 a.m., and I hadn't talked to Natalia all fucking day. I was getting angrier by the second, and didn't know if I would strangle her when I saw her, or tongue her sexy ass down.

"Alright bruh, I'm gon' head back to my crib," I said standing up and dapping Gerald up.

"Aight, don't be a stranger homie," he replied, and I nodded.

As I walked out, I saw Bianca putting her duffle bag into the back-seat of her car. I hadn't seen or talked to her in forever. She looked beautiful, but that was nothing new.

"Have a goodnight," I said as I walked by.

"Julius?" she said, and closed her car door. She ran over towards me and wrapped her arms around my neck.

"I guess you miss me," I chuckled.

"You know I did," she said as she pulled back and stared up into my eyes. "You moved back?" she asked.

"Nah, just in town to handle some business," I replied, licking my lips.

"Want to hang out?" she half smiled.

"Why not, we used to be cool, right?" I smiled.

"Nigga we were more than cool," she rolled her eyes playfully.

She followed me in her car to my old house I had before moving. Once we got inside, I started rolling some blunts as we sparked conversation.

"So how is Charleston?" Bianca asked as she lay across the bed.

"It's everything I thought it would be," I replied, lighting the blunt.

"Is that right. Did you guys have your baby yet?"

"Nah, he should be here later this week though," I replied, taking a pull.

"I missed you, Julius."

"Come show me how much," I smiled, and so did she.

She walked over to me, and straddled my lap. I slid her panties to the side, and plunged two fingers in her. I could tell that she hadn't been touched in a while. She dipped her tongue in my mouth, and we kissed as I fingered her pussy. Bianca was the only girl outside of Natalia that I would kiss, only because we'd been in a relationship for two years.

"I'm cumming Julius," she said calmly in between kisses.

Once she released, she sucked her juices off my fingers. She then dropped to her knees, and pulled my dick out. I removed my t-shirt as I watched her work her magic on my dick. Bianca knew how I liked my dick sucked, just from being with me for so long.

"Damn," I said as I felt myself on the verge of nutting.

She sped up, and I exploded in her mouth. She stood up, and then climbed on top of me. I stopped her, and then reached for a condom to put on. She didn't complain like most bitches, which was a relief. She slid down on my pole, and slightly winced in pain. Her pussy was snug as hell, and I knew nobody had been in it.

"You tight and wet, Bianca. Fuck," I moaned as she slowly bounced on my dick.

I sat up and took her hard nipples into my mouth, as she continued to wind her hips on my dick. I laid back down, and gripped her waist tightly.

"I'm cumming again. Fuck. I love you Ju!" she moaned as she came again.

I flipped her on all fours, and then slid into her from behind. I reached around to grab her neck as I plowed into her walls. I watched her ass jiggle, and knew I was about to explode.

"Mmm. Fuck," I said in a low tone.

"I'm cumming again daddy! Fuck!" Bianca moaned as she threw it back, which made me bust hard as hell.

I leaned down, and kissed her cheek from behind. I slowly pulled my dick out, making her moan. I went to the bathroom to flush the condom and take a shower. When I walked out, Bianca was knocked out, and still the position I left her in. I climbed into the bed and checked my phone; still nothing from Natalia.

Me: We over. Once the baby is born, we can just co-parent.

I sent that shit knowing I didn't mean it, but hoping it would get her attention. I needed to hear her voice. I looked at the gift I bought her, and shook my head before putting it away.

I woke up in the middle of the night, and it seemed as if someone had dumped a bucket of water in the bed. I pulled the covers back to see the sheets were soaked. Pain shot through my body as I realized I was going into labor. I ferociously tapped Frank on his back, to wake him.

"What, Nat? What's up?" he said, looking over his shoulder.

"The baby is coming!" I yelled. I had never been so scared in my life. This was a time where I missed my mommy.

Frank hopped up and threw on a t-shirt. He slipped on some jeans, and then helped me to the car. We already had a bag prepared for this day, so it was quick.

Me: I know we're over. I broke up with you remember? Co-parenting is fine. I'm in labor, headed to St. Vincent.

"Aahhhh!" I groaned in pain.

"Relax babe, just breathe. We almost there!" Frank shouted.

I started taking deep breaths to calm down, and soon enough we pulled up to the hospital. Frank hopped out and ran in to get someone to help me out the car. A couple nurses ran out with a wheelchair, and helped me get in it.

"Natalia!"

I looked over to see Julius running up, and Frank glaring at him. Julius looked so sexy, even though he wasn't even dressed up. He had on black jeans, a white t-shirt, and his all white Jordan 11's. His medium-sized chain swung from his neck, and his matching bracelet glistened. He had a fresh fade, and his caramel complexion was flawless as usual. His full lips made my mouth water. He was walking over with so much swag, even though he wasn't even trying. He bent down and kissed my lips once he neared me.

"Aye nigga! That's not your girl no more!" Frank yelled.

Julius smirked at him as they both followed the nurse who was pushing me into the hospital.

Once I was all set up, they realized it was already time to push. I was crying because there was no time to give me an epidural for the pain. This was about to be all-natural, and after all the videos I'd seen of natural births, I wanted no part of it.

"Okay, both of you can't come in the delivery room. I asked Ms. Thomas who she would like, and she asked for Julius Tate," I heard the nurse outside saying.

"This is bullshit!" I heard Frank yell.

Once they got Julius in the proper attire, he entered the room with me. He walked over and held my hand as I breathed heavily.

"Okay Ms. Thomas, let's get the first push," the doctor said. I squeezed down on Julius' hand as I pushed with all my might. "Perfect. Another one," he added.

I pushed again, and then once more before the baby was out. I felt like I was going to faint. Julius smiled and leaned down to kiss my lips once again. I let go of his hand as he went to cut the umbilical chord. After the nurses cleaned him off, they brought him back in. Our baby boy, Jackson Julius Tate, was finally here. I couldn't tell who he looked like yet, but he had the exact same small nose as Julius.

We were going to make him a Julius Jr., but Julius said he didn't want his son to be like him. I thought that was a good idea, so I agreed.

After Julius held him for a little bit, we laid him in the little plastic crib-like thing to rest. The nurse entered the room to see if I wanted Frank to come in at this point. She said he was hounding them to come in and see me. I felt bad and was gonna let him, but Julius told her no.

"Natalia, I don't want to co-parent baby girl," Julius said, grabbing my hand.

"Do you honestly love me, Julius?" I asked, and he nodded.

"Yeah ma, I was going crazy looking for you," he smiled, and so did I.

"Will you come back to South Carolina with me?" he asked.

I turned away from him, and stared at the wall. "I don't know. That video was-"

"Will you marry me, Natalia Thomas?"

I snapped my neck to look at him, and he was smiling with a big beautiful diamond ring. I reached out for it, and he moved it away.

"Is that a yes?" he smiled.

"Yes, I will," I smiled, and he slid the ring on my finger. He stood up and kissed my lips. "You knew I was gonna say yes," I replied, staring at the ring. "How many carats is this?" I inquired.

"11, cost me a lot of damn money," he chuckled.

"Good," I replied and we laughed.

I ended up having to stay in the hospital for a couple days, and Frank was blowing my damn phone up. Julius was getting angrier and angrier. I had to beg him several times not to go and fuck Frank up.

As we were packing up to leave, my phone buzzed again and I rolled my eyes. When I reached for it, Julius grabbed it from the hospital table. He saw who it was, then handed it back to me. I looked and saw it was Lucy.

Lucy Bff: I can't wait to meet little Jackson!

Me: He's soooo cute! He looks like Julius.

Lucy Bff: I thought you said you couldn't tell.

Me: His features are coming in now.

Lucy Bff: Oh when you coming back, I have an ultra sound appointment.

Me: In three days.
Lucy Bff: Yes!

I put my phone away, kissed Julius, and then we headed out with our baby in tow.

We would be flying back to South Carolina in a couple days, and a part of me couldn't wait. We didn't leave right away, because the airline said Jackson needed to be at least two weeks old.

I finished feeding my baby, and put him in the little cheap crib we bought. It was just to tide him over until we got home to his real room. Frank had finally stopped bothering me, but I still felt bad. He was always there for me, and I felt as if I shitted on him yet again.

Julius had to return to South Carolina, because he had business to handle. He wasn't going to go, but I assured him that I would be okay. I didn't want him missing anything important, when Jackson and I would be coming in a couple days anyway.

I was beat, so I decided to go ahead and take a nap while Jackson was asleep. I learned from my friend Paula back in South Carolina that it's good to have the same sleep schedule as the baby. I took my baby monitor to the bedroom, and sat it on the dresser after turning it all the way up. As soon as my head hit the pillow, I was out like a light.

"Wake yo ass up!"

I opened my eyes and realized I was staring down the barrel of a gun. I jumped back, and saw it was Greg holding it.

9 781966 375050